5-08 *

WITHDRAWN

A LIGHT
in the
DARKNESS

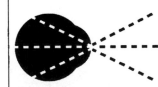

This Large Print Book carries the
Seal of Approval of N.A.V.H.

A LIGHT
in the
DARKNESS

Marilyn Prather

Thorndike Press • Waterville, Maine

Published in 2003 by arrangement with Marilyn Prather.

Thorndike Press® Large Print Candlelight Series.

The tree indicium is a trademark of Thorndike Press.

The text of this Large Print edition is unabridged. Other aspects of the book may vary from the original edition.

Set in 16 pt. Plantin.

Printed in the United States on permanent paper.

Library of Congress Cataloging-in-Publication Data

Prather, Marilyn.
    A light in the darkness / Marilyn Prather.
      p. cm.
    ISBN 0-7862-5465-3 (lg. print : hc : alk. paper)
    1. Women marine biologists — Fiction. 2. Missing children — Fiction. 3. Large type books. I. Title.
PS3566.R273L54 2003
813'.54—dc21   2003047849

To Susan Krinard and Ruth Westman,
who wouldn't let me give up and
encouraged me every step of the way

and

To Katherine Garnett,
a truly gifted poet

As the Founder/CEO of NAVH, the only national health agency solely devoted to those who, although not totally blind, have an eye disease which could lead to serious visual impairment, I am pleased to recognize Thorndike Press★ as one of the leading publishers in the large print field.

Founded in 1954 in San Francisco to prepare large print textbooks for partially seeing children, NAVH became the pioneer and standard setting agency in the preparation of large type.

Today, those publishers who meet our standards carry the prestigious "Seal of Approval" indicating high quality large print. We are delighted that Thorndike Press is one of the publishers whose titles meet these standards. We are also pleased to recognize the significant contribution Thorndike Press is making in this important and growing field.

Lorraine H. Marchi, L.H.D.
Founder/CEO
NAVH

Chapter One

As Susan Miles drove along Main Street in Gull Harbor, she noted that the quiet seaside village looked much the same as it had the last time she'd visited.

It was raining, just as it had been that day seventeen years ago when she and her parents had come up from Pitston Bay to watch the annual sailboat regatta. A nuisance rain, the natives called it. Hardly enough to make you don your trench coat, but just enough to make the wipers squeak with every pass across the windshield of your car.

Susan didn't care. She loved the showers that frequented the coast this season of the year. She loved the ocean, too, with its beige sand beaches and rocky shoreline. And she loved the dune grass, the way the wind soughed through it on blustery September evenings.

Halfway down Main Street, she pulled her blue Subaru wagon into a parking space beside a building marked HIGGINS

AGENCY. When she got out of her car, damp, cool air hit her cheeks. The sky was burdened with dark clouds. Few people were on the sidewalks for midday, but lights shone brightly from inside the building.

Susan made a dash for the door. Not surprisingly, the office was almost empty. One middle-aged woman sat at a desk near the front. She was thumbing idly through a magazine.

Susan approached and the woman glanced up with a bored expression. "What can I do for you?" she asked.

There wasn't a nameplate on the desk, but Susan thought the woman must be a receptionist. "I'm Susan Miles, and I'm renting the cottage at twenty-five Quay Road."

The receptionist frowned up at Susan, as though she had said something displeasing. She pushed a strand of gray hair back from her face with an impatient gesture. Then she riffled through a stack of papers on her desk. "Here it is." Shoving the piece of paper toward Susan, she said, "You'll be living in the cottage alone?"

"Yes." Susan returned the woman's cool gaze. "Is that a problem?"

"No. Just making sure we've got your

lease right. You're paid up, I see. I'll get the keys."

Susan watched as the woman rose and went to a large cabinet in the back of the office. Glancing out the window at the rain, she thought a cup of tea would be nice — and wondered if all the business people in Gull Harbor were as congenial as Ms. No-name. Then she reminded herself that it was typical of the area for locals to be distant with strangers.

But when the woman returned with the keys, her eyes seemed to stare through Susan. It made her uncomfortable. "Here you are."

Susan took the keys the woman offered.

"This one's for the back door." The woman pointed to the smaller of the two keys. After a long pause, she asked, "Aren't you afraid to live out there by yourself?"

The question was unexpected. Susan almost replied that she would think Gull Harbor must be one of the safest places in the world for a woman to live alone. Instead, she said, "No. Should I be?"

The receptionist's mouth twitched up in a brief smile. "I suppose not. You'll need to sign your lease." She gave Susan the document.

Susan knew she should read it, but she

wasn't much in the mood. She went ahead and signed it with the pen the woman handed her.

"This is your copy." The woman tore off the top sheet, giving Susan the yellow sheet underneath.

"Thank you," Susan said. When the receptionist didn't reply, she started for the door. Remembering something, she decided it was worth the risk of asking one question of the dour woman. "Is there a place nearby where I could get a cup of tea?"

The receptionist nodded. "Gull Café is up Main Street just a block."

Susan's hand was on the doorknob when she heard the woman clear her throat.

"Or you could try Bears' Tea Party. It's the other way about a block."

The note of sarcasm in the receptionist's voice made Susan turn around. "Bears' Tea Party? Is it a tearoom?"

"Ha!" The woman snorted. "Call it anything you want. A tearoom. An antiques shop. A toy store. If you ask me, it's mostly junk."

"Thanks for the tip. I'll try it." Susan tossed a smile the receptionist's way, but the gesture was lost on the woman, whose head was bowed again over her magazine.

Outside on the street it wasn't as blustery as before, and Susan decided to walk the short distance to Bears' Tea Party. She tilted her face up, glad for the cool drops of rain that hit her face. Her skin had been too dry the four years she'd lived away from the coast. Her naturally curly hair had gone straight too.

Susan was forced to acknowledge that she'd never quite come to terms with the arid plains of Oklahoma. Touching her hair, she noticed a certain springiness; the curls were coming back. It was a good thing, because she wasn't one to fuss with her hair and face. She didn't care to wear a lot of makeup. Now she wouldn't need to; the moisture was sure to put color in her cheeks.

A sandwich-board sign on the sidewalk announced BEARS' TEA PARTY with pretty pink letters and brightly painted bears and teacups.

A bell tinkled overhead when Susan opened the door. There was a rich cinnamon scent in the air, and everywhere she looked there were bears. They seemed to fill each nook and crevice of the tiny store, lining shelves in neat rows, sitting on tiny wicker chairs in every corner.

There were other toys too, assorted

11

stuffed animals as well as a nice mix of antique glass and metalware. The place had a cluttered appearance, Susan had to admit, but she wouldn't label it "junky" as the receptionist had.

A plump, silver-haired woman came rushing out from the back of the store.

"Oh, my dear," she said, stopping short in front of her. She looked Susan over from head to toe. "You are soaked, aren't you?"

The greeting and the warmth in the woman's eyes were a welcome contrast to the receptionist's brusque manner. "I don't mind the rain," Susan said, smiling.

The older woman smiled in return. Then the pleasant expression was replaced by a confused one. "Do I know you, dear?"

"I'm afraid not. I just arrived in Gull Harbor."

"Oh. A stranger to our fair village."

It sounded just like the quaint sort of comment Susan might expect. "Not exactly a stranger. I'm originally from Pitston Bay."

"It's a lovely town." The woman nodded. "I visited there once. I'm from North Carolina myself."

That explained the woman's friendly demeanor. "Have you lived in Gull Harbor long?" Susan asked.

"About five years. Everyone in town calls me Anna, though my full name is Annabelle Winston. And what's your name, dear?"

"Susan Miles."

"A nice name." Anna beamed. "Now what may I do for you today?"

"The receptionist at Higgins Agency told me about your tearoom."

Anna's bushy eyebrows raised in a surprised look. "That would be Marion. She's not much for small talk, would you say?"

"Not much," Susan agreed diplomatically.

"Follow me." Anna led Susan through a doorway into an alcove about the same size as the salesroom. "Welcome to Bears' Tea Party," she said. She made a sweeping gesture and motioned for Susan to sit down at a table with a lace cloth. A pink glass vase full of daisies stood in the middle of the table.

After Susan was settled in the chair, Anna said, "We have regular tea, cinnamon tea, and our own special blend of lemon grass and mint."

"The special blend sounds good."

"And to go with the tea we have fresh biscuits and honey or raspberry turnovers baked fresh this morning."

Though she hadn't thought of eating,

Susan had to concede the baked goods sounded tempting. "A raspberry turnover, Anna."

Anna folded her hands together. "A wise choice," she said solemnly, then hurried off.

Left to herself, Susan looked around the small room. In one corner was a miniature table. Seated around it were four teddy bears, each dressed in frilly finery.

Susan got up and went over to the table. Kneeling beside it, she saw that each bear had his own tea service, a delicate cup and saucer. She picked up a saucer. Its rim was painted with tiny red rosebuds and green leaves.

"I see you're getting acquainted with Mathilde and Benjamin."

Anna's voice from behind made Susan turn around. The older woman had a wide smile on her face.

Setting down the tray she held in her hands, Anna came over to the bears' table. Leaning close, she said in a whisper, "They love to meet people, you know, Benjamin and Mathilde, Gertrude and Sylvester." Her hand rested on the head of each bear in turn as she "introduced" them.

Susan observed the soft look on Anna's face. *Anna thinks the bears are real — like people,* she thought. "I'm pleased to make your acquaintance, Benjamin. And you, too, Mathilde, Gertrude, and Sylvester." She couldn't believe she was *talking* to stuffed animals! But hadn't she done that as a child? Why should she feel silly about it now?

Getting up, Susan started back to her table, where the tray sat. Anna followed. "There's a tea ball inside," Anna explained as she placed a ceramic pot in front of Susan. Next came a cup and saucer, a larger version of the ones at the bears' table, then the turnover. The pastry was dusted with powdered sugar.

"Thank you, Anna." Susan lifted the lid on the pot. "Mmm. The tea smells wonderful."

"I hope you enjoy it." Anna looked satisfied. "Will you be working in Gull Harbor?"

Susan held the teapot poised in mid-air. Several seconds passed before she answered. "I'm here to do research on a book," she said finally.

"You're a writer? How exciting."

Susan regarded Anna's eager expression. *Not so exciting when you have no guarantee of selling the book,* she wanted to say. "I will be looking for some part-time employment, though," she confessed.

"What kind might you be looking for?"

For a moment, Susan had the notion that Anna was going to offer her a job. "Whatever I can get, I'm afraid. I was a reporter for a newspaper the past four years, but I doubt —"

"How wonderful you should say that!" Anna interrupted excitedly. "Our own *Gull Beacon* has an opening for a reporter. The editor is such a nice young man and he's unattached, dear," Anna added in a lowered voice.

Susan paused again in the midst of stirring sugar into her tea. She'd just gotten into town. She hadn't seen her rental cottage yet. And here Anna was telling her about a job that sounded ideal — never mind that the editor was "nice" and "unattached." Did she want to pursue it?

When she didn't reply, Anna volunteered, "I'll give you the address in case you want to inquire. I wouldn't wait too long. I believe the newspaper office is open until five o'clock today," she added expectantly. Taking a scrap of paper from her apron, Anna wrote on it and handed it to Susan.

"I appreciate the information, Anna." Susan took the piece of paper, folded it, and stuffed it into her purse.

The bell jangled from the other room and Anna excused herself. Susan leaned back in her chair, sighing. She was in no condition for an interview today, but it might not hurt to stop by the *Beacon* office and set up an appointment.

Carefully she cut one of the corners of the turnover. Steam came out of the hot pastry. She let it cool for a moment, then lifted a forkful to her mouth.

Sounds from the other room drew her attention and she couldn't resist a peek around the corner of the alcove. A tall man with a rangy build had come into the shop. He had a black slicker on, and as he clumped loudly across the floor, Susan saw he wore heavy combat-style boots. He hardly seemed the sort to frequent a shop that sold fuzzy teddy bears and dainty tea sets. The idea made her stifle a giggle.

But when she glanced Anna's way and saw the unmistakable look of unease on the older woman's face, Susan's amusement faded.

Her years as a reporter had taught her to read faces, and Susan knew she wasn't wrong. Anna feared the man for some reason, and for a heart-thudding second, Susan imagined he must be a robber.

Maybe he had a gun concealed in his slicker, visible only to Anna.

It soon became apparent the man didn't have robbery on his mind, and Susan chided herself for her overactive imagination. Still, she couldn't stop watching. The man and Anna were talking in low tones. There seemed a sense of urgency about the conversation, though Susan couldn't make out what the man or Anna was saying.

Anna stepped behind a counter and came out with a wrapped package. What she said this time reached Susan's ears. "It's all there."

The man grabbed the parcel from Anna's hands without a response.

He must be an unhappy customer, Susan decided. Maybe there'd been a mix-up in something he'd bought. Yet she couldn't quite convince herself of it as she saw the man stalk out of the shop, especially when she peered Anna's way. The older woman was slumped against the wall, fingers pressed to her temples.

Susan tried to turn her attention back to her food, but her appetite was gone. Anna appeared to be a kindly woman. Why would anyone want to deal harshly with her? It didn't make Susan feel any better to think that the man had appeared downright menacing in his manner.

Moments later, Anna reappeared at Susan's table. "Is the tea and pastry to your satisfaction?" There was a tremor in her voice.

"It's very good." Susan put down her fork with a bite of turnover still on it. She met Anna's eyes. They were large with fear. She wanted to ask about the man, but she couldn't bring herself to. Busying herself with her wallet, she said, "I guess I wasn't as hungry as I'd thought."

"That's no problem, dear. I'll wrap it for you." Without waiting for a reply, Anna picked up the plate and rushed off.

When she returned, Anna handed Susan a foil packet; she seemed a bit more composed.

"How much do I owe you, Anna?"

"Just a dollar seventy-five."

"That's very reasonable." Susan smiled tentatively, hoping to help ease the older woman's discomfort.

Anna's mouth finally curved up in a small smile. "Will you come again, Susan?"

"I will. I promise to come again very soon." Susan handed Anna the money, then shrugged into her coat.

"I'll introduce you to all my friends."

Anna's hands fluttered in the air, indicating the dozens of bears scattered around the shop.

"If they're as charming as Benjamin, Mathilde, Gertrude, and Sylvester, then I'll look forward to it."

That must have pleased Anna, for her smile widened. As she accompanied Susan to the door, she chatted about the weather, remarking that there'd been an extraordinary amount of rain the past summer.

After exchanging good-byes, Susan stepped out onto the sidewalk, almost hating to leave Anna. As the door closed, she couldn't resist glancing back. Anna was in the window of the shop, bent over a white bear that sported a red bow tie. Her lips were moving; it was obvious she was talking to the bear.

The scene struck Susan as sad. Anna appeared vulnerable, perhaps naïve. Was she perceived as an easy target by those who enjoyed preying on others not able to defend themselves? It was a troubling thought, but Susan knew that kind of thing happened only too often.

"I must be crazy," Susan muttered to herself just before she pushed open the door with the words *Gull Beacon* stenciled on it. She'd spent the better part of an hour sitting in her car, debating whether or not to stop in at the newspaper office.

Immediately she regretted her decision. The office was tiny and cluttered and it bore the faint odor of ink. The *Gull Beacon* was obviously a small operation. But it wasn't the size or condition of the place that bothered Susan.

It was the fact that there seemed to be no receptionist on duty, as she'd expected. There seemed to be no one there at all except for the young man seated at one of the two desks. He eyed her curiously over the rim of his glasses. "May I help you?" he asked.

Susan fingered the folded note she'd taken from her purse. Anna had written the name Paul Stuart on it. Susan had more than a suspicion that the man she was facing was Paul Stuart, editor of the *Gull Beacon*.

Should she bolt from the place now without answering him? Or stammer an apology that she must have the wrong address? She was acutely aware of the rumpled condition of her clothing.

But as the man she assumed to be Paul Stuart got up from his desk and walked over to her, she noticed that his white shirt was in worse shape than her trench coat. It was wrinkled enough that one might guess he had worn it to bed last night.

"My name is Susan Miles," she managed at last as he stood before her. What was there to lose now? She went on. "I understand you have an opening for reporter on the *Gull Beacon*."

The man extended his hand to her. "I'm Paul Stuart, editor of the *Beacon*."

She'd been right about him. And his handshake was firm, his fingers pleasantly warm wrapped around hers. Regarding him, she saw he wasn't much older than herself. Though she wouldn't call him drop-dead handsome, with his wavy brown hair and trim build, he was definitely attractive — even if his shirt was badly mussed.

He let go of her hand and took off his glasses. It was then she noticed that his eyes were the most striking shade of blue. "Won't you have a seat over here, Susan?" He gave her a bemused look as he motioned her to his desk.

She wondered if he found her appearance amusing. A prickle of irritation played at the back of her neck. "My intention today was to set up an appointment for an interview. I just arrived in town and I don't have my résumé with me."

"Well, you're in the office and I don't have any interviews scheduled this afternoon," he said laconically, "so we might as well talk for a few minutes."

Maybe he had nothing better to do with his time, she thought, certain he had no intention of seriously considering her for the reporter position.

"I assume you have experience in news reporting. Why else would you be here?" He grinned at her as he settled himself behind his desk and picked up a pen.

Susan straightened, determined not to give him the satisfaction of thinking he'd flustered her. "I was employed as a reporter for the *Tulsa Evening Star* for four years," she replied evenly.

This time Paul straightened. His hand gripped the pen tighter. "Tulsa as in Oklahoma?"

"Yes." It made her feel a little smug to see his surprise.

"What brings you to Gull Harbor? Surely not the prospect of working for the *Beacon*." He carefully unscrewed the cap on his pen, then slowly screwed it on again.

"I have a degree in zoology with a minor in journalism. I moved here to do research for a book on marine flora and fauna in

North Atlantic estuaries and tide pools." Susan knew she must sound a bit pompous, but she enjoyed the way Paul's eyes widened when she told him her purpose for moving here.

"A noble reason," he admitted, bringing one hand up to smooth back his hair. "But why do you want to work for the *Beacon*?"

"I enjoy reporting, and I believe my credentials are well-suited to a position that requires coverage of a wide variety of stories." She didn't add that she badly needed the money, that she hadn't received a contract on the book in question, only the interest of a publisher who happened to be the very good friend of her managing editor at the *Star*.

Paul leaned forward. "The position with the *Beacon* is part-time, Susan. We publish once a week and we'd like to hire someone who's capable of covering a variety of assignments, as you said. Everything from the town's annual Harvest Festival to a speech on the Commons by the governor. We'd also prefer the applicant have experience in news photography."

"I was a general reporter for the *Star*, and on a number of occasions I photographed the scene of the story. I'll be doing my own photography on the book I'm researching."

"Good." Paul looked satisfied. "Your experience sounds like it fits our needs, though of course I'll need to see your résumé." He reached in a desk drawer and withdrew a piece of paper. "Here's an application to fill out if you're interested in the position. I'd like to have it back by Tuesday, then we can talk in more specific terms."

Susan blinked as he slid the application across the desk. Everything was happening so fast. Soon she might be an employee of the *Gull Beacon* — if she wanted to be. "I can come in on Tuesday," she told him.

"Great! Could you stop by the office at one o'clock?"

She saw that Paul's glasses had slipped partway down his nose. He pushed them up with an impatient gesture that she found cute. She decided that it might be fun working in a cubbyhole of an office with him. Pushing aside images of cute, she said, "One o'clock would be fine."

He got up and walked her to the door. "I hope you don't mind rainy weather."

Susan paused on the threshold of the door. "I love rain. I'm originally from Pitston Bay."

His face registered surprise again. "Is that so? I grew up in Detroit."

It was her turn to be surprised. She might have taken him for a native. "Thank you for your time, Paul," she said, stepping outside.

He nodded in return, then closed the door between them. It wasn't until she was almost to her car that Susan realized the rain had stopped and the sun was shining. What she'd told Paul about rain was true. But just now, she couldn't help but believe the clearing sky was a good omen.

Chapter Two

After a quick stop at a seafood restaurant for a takeout bowl of clam chowder, Susan headed east from town. The drive to the cottage on Quay Road took longer than she expected. It turned out that the house was set off by itself, flanked by maple and spruce trees.

As she pulled into the gravel lane leading up to the cottage, she thought of Marion's question: "Aren't you afraid to live there by yourself?" Was there a reason to be? Susan had to wonder once more. The cottage looked snug; the ocean was at her back door. The trees provided sturdy shelter in front.

She turned the motor off and rolled down the car window. Though the ocean wasn't visible through the trees, Susan could hear it, hear the faint, steady beat of the waves against the shore.

She sat a minute longer, then got out, juggling the covered container of chowder in one hand and a suitcase in the other. A cobblestone path led up to the front door of the cottage.

Fitting the key in the lock, Susan pushed the door open. Another odor assailed her; the cottage reeked of mildew, evidence that it must have been vacant for some time. A good airing of the place would remedy the problem.

Though the rooms were sparsely furnished, the living room and bedroom were fairly large and there was a tiny kitchen. With a few visits to Bears' Tea Party for the purchase of a couple of stuffed toys and a vase or two, the cottage might be upgraded to cozy.

Susan put the chowder on the kitchen counter and caught a glimpse of the ocean through the small window over the sink. After dropping her suitcase off in the bedroom and retrieving the rest of her luggage from the car, she opened all the windows and went out the back door to the narrow deck that ran the length of the cottage.

The ocean and secluded stretch of beach were the main reasons she'd agreed to rent the cottage sight unseen. Leaning over the railing of the deck, she wasn't sorry. The roar of the waves seemed to envelop her as sunlight and cloud shadows played on the water.

She picked up her bowl of chowder and walked down to the beach. Sitting cross-legged on the sand, Susan ate while a gull circled lazily overhead. Positive that she'd never tasted chowder that good before, she wondered if it was because she'd been away from the coast for so long. The sea was in her blood; landlocked Oklahoma had only made her yearn for the sights and sounds of home.

Susan felt more at peace than she had in a very long time. She licked the spoon, savoring the last bit of chowder. If Paul offered her the job of reporter and if, eventually, her book got written and published, she might consider buying a cottage like this one. She could fix it up just the way she wanted. Whimsically she thought that she might even decide to live in Gull Harbor forever.

For now, there were more practical matters to consider — such as unpacking. Sighing, she got up and went back inside. Tomorrow there would be time to walk along the beach and see what lay beyond those clumps of trees obscuring her view to the north and south.

Tomorrow too she would see about renting a small sailboat or skiff to explore the more rugged shoreline farther north.

The prospect of being on the water again, of discovering the tide pools that dotted the rocky crevices of the coast, sent a shiver of anticipation up her spine.

The next day dawned clear and cloudless, and Susan wakened, refreshed. After a breakfast of instant oatmeal that she'd remembered to pack, she put a roll of film in her camera and headed for the beach.

She shot a few pictures of the dunes and tall grass that grew along the sandy shore. She had just lowered her camera to gaze out at the surf when she sensed that she wasn't alone.

"Can that be Susan Smiles?"

Susan gasped, nearly dropping her camera. No one had called her that since she was a senior in high school. She turned to the man who had come up beside her. "Rodney?" she asked, peering up into his face. But she knew it was him from the tilt of his head.

Rodney Silvers was a former classmate from Pitston High. Rodney had been a jock, voted Prom King, Most Popular, and, in her mind, Most Cocky. His father owned the very prosperous Silvers Seafood Sauce Company.

By contrast, she'd been voted Most Studious, known as the girl who would rather chase bugs than boys and who never went anywhere without her swamp waders. Her father had been Pitston's town clerk for years, a respectable position that paid a less-than-respectable salary.

She hadn't known Rodney well in school, but she knew he'd had plenty of confidence — and plenty of girls practically begging him for dates.

Had he changed? It was doubtful, she thought. He was grinning at her. And what was he doing here, on her stretch of beach, a good distance from Pitston?

"I hope I didn't scare you." His hands were on his hips. He wore a sleeveless red T-shirt and matching shorts. His biceps still bulged and his face was as tanned and handsome as she remembered, though a bit more mature looking.

Susan's cheeks suddenly felt warm. She couldn't be blushing, could she? Surely it must be the sun.

"Are you okay, Susan?" His grin widened.

"I'm fine," she said too quickly. "It's just that I thought I was alone. Then when you called me —"

"Susan Smiles," he put in just as fast. "I started following you as soon as you came out of the Lambert cottage. To see if it was really you."

"The Lambert cottage?"

Rodney laughed. "That's what people around here call it." He stooped over, picked up a handful of sand, and let it sift slowly through his fingers. "A woman named Chris Lambert and her daughter, Amy, lived there. That is, until a short while ago."

"I hope they enjoyed the cottage as much as I'm sure I'm going to."

His expression darkened. "It isn't likely."

"Why?" There seemed a sudden chill in the air; Susan realized the sun had slipped behind a cloud.

"Amy disappeared off this beach. According to her mother, she went out to play, and a few minutes later, she vanished. Just like that." He snapped his fingers, squinting up at the sun. "That would be three months ago now."

"No," Susan whispered. She clutched her sides unconsciously, as though she could protect her heart from the invisible blow Rodney had unknowingly inflicted.

"Hey, Susan, what's the matter?" Rodney's hand flicked her arm. His face wore a scowl.

Susan turned away from him. What could

she say? *Joey,* her mind screamed. *Poor little Joey. Poor Stephanie too.* "Nothing," she said aloud. "It's nothing, Rodney."

"Are you sure?" He looked skeptical. "I didn't mean to upset you."

Susan's tongue passed over her lips. They felt dry. "I guess it's just that . . . whenever a child disappears, it's so . . . tragic."

"Yeah, sure," he agreed, but his voice was flat, with no hint of emotion. "If it's any comfort, the authorities believe Amy's father took her." Rocking back on his heels, Rodney clasped his hands in front of him. It served to better show off his muscles. "There'd been a messy divorce, though everyone figured Chris would get custody."

Susan let out a shaky breath. "Did you know the couple and their daughter?"

He glanced away. "I live just down the block, so to speak. I'm your neighbor." He gave Susan a brief smile. "I dated Chris a few times after the divorce. That's all."

When he didn't offer any further information, Susan sought to change the subject. She knew what to ask. "How did you happen to move up here to Gull Harbor?"

"Well, I could ask you the same question," he shot back, that grin in place again. "I wanted to get away from the old neighborhood, play the beach bum for a while."

He had the money to do it, Susan reckoned. "No connections with the family company?"

Rodney shrugged. "Of course. I'm the P.R. man. I travel around a lot, promoting the sauce." He sounded bored. "So what exciting prospects lured you to the dinky village of Gull Harbor?"

The question begged for a witty comeback, but she couldn't think of one. "I'm here to do research for a book."

"Let me guess." Rodney broke off a piece of dune grass, drew it between his fingers, then put it in his mouth. "The subject is wolf spiders and their mating habits."

He said it as though that particular subject was distasteful, which she assumed it would be to him. "Close. You know, Rodney, I have to say I'm surprised to see you here. I thought you'd be living in Miami, riding the surf from there to St. Croix."

"Touché." He threw the piece of chewed grass aside. Looking out over the water, he got up and asked, "Were you planning on spending the day on the beach?"

It was a smooth way to duck the question, she conceded. "No. I planned to find a marina where I could rent a sailboat."

He regarded her. "Why do you want to rent a boat?"

Susan wondered why he was so curious about her when the only interest he'd ever shown her before was to give her the nickname "Susan Smiles." It must have been because she was more serious than full of smiles back then. And still was, she supposed. "To explore the shoreline farther north," she replied.

"I see." He looked thoughtful. "If it's a boat you want, my yacht is moored at my own private dock right down there." He gestured south toward the clump of trees. "You can't see it, but it's there. Seventy-five yards from my house. I call her *Silver Belle*. She has everything from bunk beds to a wet bar."

"*Silver Belle*. That's a perfect name, Rodney." He beamed at her compliment. "Thanks for the offer, but I think it'd be more practical for me to rent a skiff." She couldn't picture him pressing the *Silver Belle* into service to search for slugs and starfish.

His smile turned into a frown. He obviously wasn't used to being rejected by women. "If that's what you want." He shrugged and got up, dusting the sand off his legs.

Susan's eyes were drawn to those legs. Lean, muscular, browned by the sun. Quickly she looked away. Wasn't that his intention? To show off his physique?

"Then how about if I show you around, Susan? After all, you're new to town. We could start with a tony little seafood and steak restaurant I'm acquainted with. They've got a band for dancing."

The invitation took her completely off guard. Was he asking her for a *date?* That seemed as equally impossible as the offer of his yacht, but when she looked at him he appeared sincere.

"Well, what do you say? How about Friday night? Say I pick you up at six?"

"All right," Susan heard herself reply. She had no idea why she'd accepted, and even less idea what dress she might own that would be appropriate to wear to a tony little seafood and steak place.

"Fantastic!" Rodney enthused. "Now let me point you to the nearest marina."

She felt him take hold of her arm and she let herself be steered in a northerly direction.

"Go right around those trees, Susan. Stay on the beach, and about two miles up you'll find Sam's Marina. Tell the old salt that Rodney sent you."

He gave her a tap on the arm, as though the mention of his name should be an in with Sam, the "old salt" whom she presumed owned the boat dock.

The dock wasn't hard to find, she discovered, and the beach was deserted, giving her time to contemplate her strange meeting with Rodney — and time to mull over the startling tale he had told her about the missing child. Susan looked out over the gently rolling waves of the ocean. Had Amy Lambert waded into the water and drowned? If so, wouldn't her body have washed ashore?

Was that why Marion had questioned the fact she would be living at the cottage alone? Susan shivered despite the heat of the sun, and she tried to put the subject out of her mind, though she was sure to think of it later.

At the marina she met a grizzled man who looked as if he'd spent his share of time on the waves. He introduced himself to her as Sam.

When she told him she was looking for a sailboat to rent, he told her to follow him to one of several piers where numerous vessels were moored. "This is the *Anne Marie*," he said, indicating a small white skiff. "She's a good little sailboat. Should serve you real well." He tucked his thumbs through two of the loops on his shabby trousers and gave Susan a toothy smile.

She regarded the boat. It looked seaworthy enough, and it had a motor as well as sails. A good thing, since the air could suddenly turn calm. "The *Anne Marie* should do. Could I rent her for a month to begin with?"

Sam nodded. "We'll go inside and fix up the contract and she's all yours."

Susan liked Sam. He reminded her of the man who ran the marina in Pitston where her parents had kept a small boat years ago.

The marina was a low, rambling building. Colorful buoys hung from the ceiling. One handwritten sign advertised bait for sale; another hung over a lunch counter, announcing the daily special as fish and chips. Susan suspected it was the only special Sam had, but the smell was inviting.

While Sam filled out the paperwork, she browsed through a rack of brochures and found a map of the coastline north and south of Gull Harbor.

"Take whatever you need," Sam offered,

glancing up from the counter where he worked.

Susan opened the map and examined it. She immediately took note of an area designated Barr Estuary. An "X" farther north on the map was marked Rocky Pointe Lighthouse. That might bear checking out too, she thought.

Sam finished the contract and Susan signed it. She debated for a minute whether to get some fish and chips for her first outing on the *Anne Marie* and was about to ask Sam for an order when she heard someone call her name.

Looking around, she was astonished to see Paul heading her way. It was turning out to be a day for surprises. "Paul! What are you doing here?" Instantly she wished she could take the words back. Why should she be amazed to see her possible employer at the marina?

"Occasionally I like to go sailing," he returned with a smile.

She thought he looked unusually pleased to see her, though she couldn't imagine why. Like herself, he was dressed quite differently than the day before. Though he wasn't muscle-bound like Rodney, his tan crew top and fitted jeans complemented his build. "That's just what I was about to do," she said at last. "I've rented a boat so I can explore the coastline."

"A sailboat?" he asked.

"Yes. She's called the *Anne Marie*."

"Mine's the *Beacon Too*. T, double O," he spelled out in explanation.

"I might have guessed." Susan had to laugh.

Paul made no move to leave and Susan felt suddenly shy under the steady blue gaze of his eyes. "I guess I had better be going now," she said finally.

"Where is it you're going?"

He seemed as full of questions as Rodney. She got out her map. If he really wanted to know, she would be specific. "I thought I'd see what Barr Estuary has to offer, to start."

"The estuary." Paul said it almost excitedly. "I go there often to hike . . . and sometimes to meditate," he added softly.

Susan peered up at him from under lowered lashes. A man who liked to seek out quiet places — to meditate. There might be a lot more to this Paul Stuart than appearances suggested. "I'll be going to photograph some plants and animals, and maybe to do a bit of meditating too," she said just as softly.

"Why don't I show you around, help you

get acquainted with our local coast? The office is closed today and I was planning to go sailing myself."

Just as quickly as she'd turned down Rodney's offer, she accepted Paul's — and wondered again if she were crazy. How did it look to eagerly accept an invitation from the man who might be her boss in just a few days?

It didn't seem to bother Paul in the least. In fact, he looked even more pleased than before. She tried to convince herself that he was just being neighborly. After all, she was new to the area. And hadn't Anna pronounced him a "nice young man"? Yes, and "unattached." "I'd like to take the *Anne Marie*," she said.

"Fine, no problem." Paul peered out one of the long windows of the marina. "Looks like a breeze has come up, enough to use the sails."

The matter appeared settled and Paul started for the door. Susan followed, then stopped. The smell of frying fish reached her nose again. "Wait, I'd like to get something to eat, to take along," she added.

"Would fish and chips do?" Paul asked with a grin.

She grinned back. "Fish and chips would be great."

Sam wrapped up two orders of the fish and fries for them and gave Paul a wink that Susan interpreted as conspiratorial. Noticing that Paul winked back, she had to wonder what he was thinking.

She had no more time to ponder the matter as she followed him out the door and down to the dock where the *Anne Marie* was waiting.

The weather turned out to be perfect, with a moderate northerly wind. Seated opposite Paul in the boat, Susan duly noted that he was a competent sailor. In fact, he looked quite at home on the water.

When they were safely past the shoals that lay near shore, Susan leaned back and munched on her fish and chips, savoring the feel of ocean spray on her face.

They headed north and she got out her map, checking for Barr Estuary. It didn't take them long to reach the refuge. Paul expertly guided the small craft up the wide mouth of the estuary. On either side were expanses of dune and cord grass, emerald green against blue sky.

"It's beautiful, Paul." Immediately Susan could see rich possibilities for filling a number of pages in her research notebook.

Paul nodded, a look of satisfaction on his face. "Over there," he said, motioning toward an area of dense trees and grass, "is a nature trail. A few years ago, shortly after I moved to Gull Harbor, Barr Estuary was named a nature preserve and a series of wooden walkways was built so the public could see the beauty of the refuge up close."

"That means it's protected land," Susan offered.

Paul turned to her, a slightly troubled look creasing his brow. He pushed up his glasses, though it didn't appear to Susan that they had slipped much on his nose. "Not all of it. There's a battle going on. A developer versus the conservationists."

"The developer wants to build a shopping center?"

"Not quite." Paul maneuvered the *Anne Marie* close to shore and dropped anchor. "A condominium complex." He got out, offering his hand to Susan to help her from the boat.

His fingers enveloped hers, and she liked the feeling. She told herself not to like it too much, but she couldn't deny she was attracted to Paul. She missed the warmth when he released her hand. To hide her wayward emotions, she busied herself by taking out her camera.

They hiked for a while along the sandy

shoreline. Dunes, sculpted by the wind, rose to the west away from the flat bottom where water met land. Cord grass stood straight and proud along the ridges of the dunes.

Paul seemed in no hurry as Susan stopped to take pictures and make a few notes.

"We could spend the afternoon here, hiking the trails," he suggested, "or venture a bit farther up the coast in the *Anne Marie*. Which would you like to do, Susan?"

His eyes held hers and she found that it didn't matter much what they did. But she finally opted for the latter. "I can always come back, Paul. I'm curious to see what's along the coast."

They walked back the same way they'd come to the place where the *Anne Marie* was anchored. Paul again took Susan's hand as she got into the boat. He seemed reluctant to let go, and when she looked at him, Susan thought for a moment that she saw her own attraction mirrored in the clear depths of his eyes. It must be her imagination.

She reminded herself she wasn't in the market for a relationship — with Paul or Rodney or anyone else. That wasn't the reason she'd chosen Gull Harbor. If she allowed herself to get involved with a man she could easily end up working for, she was asking to complicate her life. Provided, of course, the feeling was mutual. A glance Paul's way found him studying her. It did nothing to dispel her discomfort.

Susan swiftly looked away. Wasn't she happy with her life the way it was? She'd dated a little during the four years she'd spent in Tulsa, mostly casual dates. She hadn't been serious about anyone there and, at the time, it had seemed a good arrangement.

They settled themselves in the hull of the small boat. Paul pulled anchor and steered the *Anne Marie* north.

Susan lifted the map. "I saw this lighthouse marked Rocky Pointe. Do you know anything about it, Paul?"

A sudden scowl creased his face. "A little," he said tersely.

Susan wondered at his reaction. "I had thought of going up there today. Is it far?"

"An hour, maybe."

"I gather you don't care for the lighthouse. Is there some reason? I've always thought lighthouses were fascinating."

"They are," he said, leaning toward her. "But this particular lighthouse is owned by a very nasty guy, someone you wouldn't want to tangle with."

That surprised her. "You mean the keeper?"

Paul shook his head. "There is no keeper now. Rocky Pointe used to be a working lighthouse. The state closed it a year or so ago. The whole property, keeper's house and all, was sold."

"Does the man who owns it, the nasty guy, live there?"

"No." Paul guided the *Anne Marie* past a shoal out into open water. Susan noted that the sandy shore was giving way to pebbly beach and outcroppings of rock.

"Why did he buy it?"

"Daryl Travers — that's his name — isn't big on conversation, Susan. Who knows why he wanted Rocky Pointe, though I've got my suspicions. One thing, it borders the property where his home sits." Paul looked away out over the expanse of ocean. Waves lapped gently around the boat.

Susan wanted to ask Paul what his suspicions were, but she refrained, wrapping her arms around her knees instead. For some reason, the wind felt more bitter along this rugged stretch of coast.

Paul turned his attention back to her. "A

citizens' group was formed. We wanted to make the lighthouse a historic landmark. But Travers got there first with his checkbook. Now there's a barbed wire fence surrounding the lighthouse and its outbuildings."

"I'd still like to see it," Susan said quietly.

"That's where we're headed." Paul gave her a slight smile.

They fell silent for several minutes, and Susan watched as Paul steered the small vessel through the water. Those troublesome feelings of attraction asserted themselves once more. Even when she lowered her eyes to consider the map, she found herself stealing glances at him.

What was it exactly about Paul that intrigued her? He wasn't all that much taller than she was. In many respects he was much like any other young, good-looking man she might happen upon. But there was something less definable about him, something a bit elusive in his manner that caught her attention.

It was evident in the way he carried himself, the way he talked, the way he looked at her. Yes, the way he was looking at her now with a sense of quiet assurance, yet there was an undercurrent of something.

Was it vulnerability, such as she'd sensed in Anna? Did he in some way remind her of herself? The air of understated confidence prevailed, to be sure, but Susan wished she could discern the other and what caused it.

One thing she was sure of: Paul Stuart inspired her trust. Somehow she wasn't surprised when she felt his hand touch her arm.

"Look, Susan."

She gazed in the direction he was pointing. A huge gray rock jutted skyward from the water not far from land. It stood like a silent guardian, a testament to the power of the sea, the waves that had washed over it through aeons of time, leaving the stone half veiled in spray. "How lovely," she whispered.

"Yes," he agreed quietly. "I thought you'd appreciate it."

Susan took out her camera. Paul maneuvered the *Anne Marie* so she could get the best angle for a picture of the rock. She shot several frames before they moved on.

"It won't be much longer now. We're nearing Rocky Pointe."

The terrain had definitely changed. The coastline here was much more dramatic and untamed, Susan observed, than the sloping stretch of beach near her cottage.

"Tell me, Paul, how did you decide to move to Gull Harbor?"

He looked thoughtful and seemed to waver for a moment before he answered. "I'd needed a change, a major one, about the time a friend of mine in Selby sent me an ad announcing the opening for editor of the *Beacon.*"

"You have a friend in Selby. That's a nice village." Susan wasn't really thinking of the picturesque town located about halfway between Pitston and Gull Harbor. She was thinking more of Paul's other words, the fact he'd needed a major change. "Didn't you like Detroit?"

"I grew up there," he said, not really answering her question. "I attended the University of Chicago, got my degree in journalism, and then went back to Detroit, where I worked at the *Free Press* for a few years."

He might be slightly older than she'd first thought, though Susan doubted he was much more than thirty. "That sounds a lot more challenging, or should I say exciting, than putting out a small weekly newspaper." She wasn't sure she'd said the right thing, but he smiled.

"It was, I have to confess. The reason I

left had nothing to do with job dissatisfaction, Susan. In fact, I was up for a promotion shortly before I gave notice."

She expected him to explain what it was that made him leave the *Free Press*, but he looked away, and when he spoke again, it was to tell her that Rocky Pointe was just ahead.

On her first glimpse of Rocky Pointe Lighthouse, Susan gasped. The tower stood perched atop a promontory that rose high above the water. It was one of the most majestic lights she had ever seen, painted in white with green trim, as were the other buildings at its base. The place didn't look abandoned. She had to give Daryl Travers that much credit. He must keep the property in good repair.

As they drew closer, Paul steered the *Anne Marie* to a bay encircled by rocky outcroppings. Immediately Susan saw the rugged shoreline was rife with tide pools. The tiny ponds glinted in the afternoon sun like beckoning jewels.

"This is perfect, Paul." She hadn't realized that she had reached for him until she felt him take her hand. "The tide pools," she added, turning to him.

Paul squeezed her hand once before letting go. "The tide pools may be perfect,

Susan, but this place isn't."

She followed his gaze to the light and then she saw the tall wire fence.

"Daryl Travers's property is surrounded by barbed wire with signs that clearly read *keep out*." Paul emphasized the words.

"Do you think he patrols the place?" Susan found herself whispering. She squinted, trying to see any movement on the property.

"I wouldn't put it past him to police the grounds."

Susan laughed nervously. The lighthouse didn't look sinister — or occupied. It looked inviting, but she had no desire to cross paths with a man who valued his privacy that much. Where they stood was well outside the bounds of his domain, though.

"They're a virtual treasure chest of marine life," she said, indicating the tide pools again. "Just what I was anticipating." What was she hoping for? That Paul would give her his blessing, say it was perfectly safe for her to come here by herself, study the flora and fauna to her heart's content?

"It's tempting, Susan, but I wouldn't risk it. *Don't* risk it."

The way he said it gave rise to that same prickle of irritation she'd felt before in his office. "Personally I don't see any danger,

Paul. What can Daryl Travers do to me down here? I don't intend to trespass on his precious place."

Paul gave her a sharp look. "I wouldn't, Susan." This time he drew the words out.

Susan returned his sharp look, crossing her arms in front of her. Why had she agreed to Paul's company anyway? If she'd known he was going to impose his opinions on her, she would have come alone. Never mind that even in her anger she found herself drawn to him. Never mind that his scowl was having the opposite effect of what he intended.

Suddenly she laughed, her tension falling away.

"What?" Paul gave her a puzzled glance, though it was obvious he was still trying to be stern.

"Nothing. Only that we're nearly arguing and we've just met — and I don't even know if you'll hire me for the reporter's job." She was aware that she was babbling, but his reply was fast and direct.

"You've got the job. Tuesday will just be a formality."

"Really?" Maybe he *was* joking.

"Yes, really." His eyes captured hers.

"Can I show you why I get so excited about tide pools, Paul?"

His reply was to allow her to lead him to one of the miniature oceans.

The pool was teeming with life. Susan knelt beside it and Paul followed suit. "Look! There's a bushy-backed sea slug."

Reason told Susan she couldn't expect Paul to be enthused over the tiny animal with reddish-brown antennae that waved like feathery plumes when a breeze stirred the water. But incredibly, he seemed to be. "Is that what it is?" Paul bent very close to the water, watching the creature until it slid out of sight beneath a stone. "I know that one." He pointed. "A starfish. And there's an anemone, right?" He grinned at her.

"That earns you an A in zoology, you know."

Paul laughed, shaking his head. "You really study all of this?" His gesture took in the smattering of pools on the ledge.

"I do," Susan replied solemnly.

"Please just choose to do it somewhere else."

There he went again, telling her what to do. And his gaze, intense and unwavering, compelled her to mutter, "All right." But she had no intention of keeping a promise made under duress. The tide pools were just too much of a temptation. She told herself that as long as she stayed well outside the fortress Daryl Travers had fashioned, she would be safe. She promptly squelched any niggling doubts to the contrary.

Chapter Three

They headed back down the coast, and Paul told her stories he'd heard from Sam, tales of shipwrecks and heroic rescues at sea during the fierce winter storms that often visited the area. But he didn't broach the subject of Daryl Travers and his lighthouse again. And Susan didn't ask. Nor did she ask any more about the reason he'd left Detroit and the *Free Press* for a one-man newsroom in Gull Harbor.

It didn't seem long at all to Susan until they were back at the marina. Explaining that he had a story to cover that evening, Paul excused himself, but not before he said he wished he had time to take her out for a bite of dinner. Another time, he promised with a smile.

Susan watched him walk away. He turned back once to wave, then got into a gray car, a small foreign model similar to hers, and was gone.

After walking back down the beach to her cottage, Susan decided to go out for a hamburger. The day before she'd noticed a fast-food place only a few miles up Quay Road from the cottage.

She brought her burger and a salad home to eat on the deck. While she looked out over the ocean and munched her dinner, she thought about the afternoon she'd just spent with Paul.

She couldn't remember when she'd enjoyed herself so much in the company of a man. Somehow it reminded her of her date with Rodney the following Friday. She wasn't especially looking forward to it, and that made her feel almost guilty.

Ten years ago, any girl at Pitston High would have gladly bartered a new wardrobe for a date with Rodney Silvers. And as gorgeous a man as Rodney still was, Susan imagined any single woman in Gull Harbor and distant points beyond would clamor for the chance to be seen with him.

Why didn't she feel any excitement? Maybe it had something to do with the condescending way he'd treated her in school. Or maybe it was because there just wasn't any chemistry between them — at least not on her part. Was it logical to think that all of a sudden he'd discovered her, found her so attractive that he wanted to take her to an upscale place for dinner and dancing?

Susan sighed. If she needed to debate about chemistry, better to consider Paul. No, better not, she told herself. First she had to get through the weekend, though she suspected Tuesday and her meeting with Paul at the office would come soon enough.

She sat on the deck until the sun had set behind her cottage, casting long shadows from the trees across the sand. She was reminded of a more disturbing reality than the emotions stirred by Paul's presence.

How long did Chris and Amy Lambert live in the Quay Road cottage? she wondered. How long before Amy's disappearance?

Susan went inside, locking the back door behind her. She turned on the lamps in the living room and bedroom. Their warm glow splashed over the woven rugs and simple pieces of furniture, but the cottage bore a certain chill.

Had Chris and Amy shared any happy times in that living room, perhaps snuggled together on the braided rug to play with a special toy?

There'd been a messy divorce, Rodney

had said. And then Amy had turned up missing.

A gust of wind blew through the still-open windows. A lamp nearly toppled over from the blast and Susan hurried to shut the windows.

She knew she should finish the unpacking she had been putting off. Without enthusiasm, she emptied two suitcases before deciding to call it a night. She could finish over the weekend. Her day at sea had made her sleepy.

After she took a quick shower and put on a fresh teddy, she got out a pair of sheets, her pillow and a coverlet. The bed was queen size. Had Chris and Amy slept peacefully there? Unfolding a pillowcase, Susan mentally shook herself. She wished that Rodney hadn't told her about the case. But it was her own question that had precipitated it.

She made the bed, turning down the coverlet. Switching off the lamp, she slipped between the clean sheets. As she lay there, more awake than she should be, Susan knew it was useless to mull over the tragedy that had happened at the cottage.

Hadn't she learned anything from the Joey Peterson case, when, as a new and unseasoned reporter, she had crossed the fragile line between objective reporting and personal involvement? Ironically she had also done some of her best work on that assignment.

Susan turned on her side, punching the pillow with her fists to plump it up. The bed was firm and comfortable; the musty smell was gone from the rooms of the cottage.

She yawned, closing her eyes. Images of Paul, Rodney, and Anna Winston and her quaint shop floated in the darkness behind her eyelids and she felt herself getting groggy. She wished for pleasant dreams, but the last thing she remembered before drifting to sleep was the sound of the wind moving through the dune grass. It wasn't the comforting sound she'd always thought it to be. Instead, the song the wind played tonight was sad and lonely.

On Tuesday, Susan dressed carefully for her meeting with Paul. She put on her tailored navy-blue suit and a crisp white blouse that she'd forced herself to iron over the weekend.

Casting a critical eye in the mirror as she applied her lipstick, Susan noted that her hair curled softly around her face. She looked presentable, she decided. No, more than presentable. Though she'd never considered herself pretty, despite frequent compliments to the contrary, she had to admit the white blouse against navy enhanced her smooth complexion and intensified the color in her cheeks.

But half an hour later, when she stepped into the newspaper office, there was a telltale nervous quiver in the pit of her stomach. It couldn't be because she feared she might be turned down for the reporter position. Paul had already assured her the job was hers.

"Susan."

She turned in the direction of Paul's voice. He was standing by a water cooler that was set in a corner of the office. He appeared relaxed, one elbow propped against the glass top of the cooler. "I see you're on time."

"Isn't a good reporter supposed to keep an eye on her watch?"

Paul strode over to her, grinning. "Always."

"Here's the application, filled out, of course, and my résumé."

He took them from her outstretched hand and motioned for her to take the chair beside his desk. Head bent, he studied her application for a few moments.

Susan discreetly studied him, liking the way his hair fell down a little onto his forehead.

From the appearance of his clothing, it seemed that he also had been busy ironing over the weekend. He had on a neatly pressed blue shirt, a shade slightly darker than his eyes. Those errant gold-rimmed glasses slipped down his nose again. Susan anticipated the gesture she took for a mannerism. When his hand didn't come up to shove the glasses back in place, she almost reached over to do the job for him.

Stop it, she chided herself.

All the while, Paul's face held a neutral expression. That was, until his eyes met hers. She could swear the color in his cheeks deepened — and it wasn't due to the sun he'd been exposed to on their outing up the coast.

He cleared his throat. "Mmmm. Everything seems to be in order. But then, I did tell you the job's yours, didn't I?" When that elicited the appropriate response, a smile from her, he continued. "I see you won a press award for a series of articles you wrote. May I ask what the subject was?"

A lump formed swiftly in Susan's throat. She fought it down, uncertain whether she could speak. "A missing child case," she said finally. She paused for another heartbeat. "The woman — Stephanie Peterson was her name — was a single mother, raising her child alone. I did several interviews with her after Joey disappeared. Joey was her son," she added, her voice almost a whisper.

"Was the boy, Joey, found?" Paul's voice was quiet too.

Susan looked down at her hands. They were clenched together in her lap. Raising her head, she met Paul's gaze. "No." For an instant she had the strange sensation that Paul could look into her head, her heart, that he understood exactly how she felt.

Paul broke eye contact first. He made a pretense of straightening one of the piles of papers on his desk. "The reporter's job doesn't pay much," he said.

"It'll pay enough. My main concern is that I'm not so busy covering stories that I won't have the time I'd like to devote to my research."

"I promise you will have the time, Susan." He leaned forward, an earnest expression on his face.

She leaned forward too. "I realize breaking news doesn't bow to a reporter's convenience."

"No, but how many breaking stories do you suppose there are in an average week in a village of one thousand people?"

Susan laughed, then grew suddenly serious. She thought of a breaking story that must have filled the front page of a good many issues of the *Gull Beacon*.

Though he didn't say so aloud, she sensed that Paul also must be thinking of Amy. He touched her briefly. "Are you all right?"

She only shook her head. "When do I start?" The words were a little choked.

"How about this Friday morning? Say around eleven o'clock?"

"Okay." It would be the same day she had a date with Rodney, but she didn't care.

"If you have time now, I'd like to show you around the office, give you an idea of how we put out a weekly newspaper here."

"Sounds good, Paul."

They both got up and he indicated the other, vacant desk. "This is yours. I got it in anticipation of hiring a reporter." His eyebrows rose.

Susan saw there was a small computer on the desk top, which had been empty the week before.

Paul went over to a file cabinet and

returned with a small stack of newspapers. He laid them on her desk. "You can take these home with you to read. Generally an issue is six to eight pages, though if it's a big news week, we might go to ten. Most of what we cover is local. When someone in town wants to read about the President's proposed budget, they buy a big-city newspaper like *The New York Times*."

Susan returned his smile. "I'm looking forward to reading these." She indicated the papers.

They moved on to the pasteup table and Paul showed her where he kept supplies. "We don't do a lot of pasteup anymore now that we've got computer graphics. See, we're not all that different from a large newsroom."

An optimistic statement if she ever heard one. "You say we. I thought it was just you."

"Did you think I ran the press too?" Paul tilted his head, eyes slanted in amusement.

"Well, I assumed. . . ." She stopped, embarrassed.

"Steven Haines is the *Beacon*'s pressman. You'll meet him soon. He's due in anytime. We've got a problem with the equipment, I'm afraid."

"Oh, no. The press is down."

Paul shrugged, nonchalant. "Nothing to get upset over. It happens all the time." He invited her to follow him. "I'll show you the beast."

They went through a doorway into a small back room. In the middle of the room sat the beast, an older model Multigraphic press.

"It's seen better days, but I think it's got a couple of years left in it," Paul said with a certain affection.

Susan smiled. The machine indeed looked as though it had seen better days. She heard someone whistling in the outer office. Turning, she saw a short, balding man bustle through the doorway.

"Steven."

"Hi, Paul." The man hurried over to Paul. Then he seemed to notice Susan. He eyed her quizzically.

"Susan, this is Steven Haines."

Steven immediately extended his hand to her. "Nice to meet you, Susan."

"Susan Miles is our new reporter."

"It's about time, Paul." Steven grinned broadly at Susan. "He's been working himself to death." Steven's head jerked in Paul's direction. "I told him what he needed was to get himself a pretty young assistant."

Paul coughed and Susan cleared her throat while Steven laughed heartily.

"Did you get the part, Steven?" Paul asked a bit too quickly.

"Got it all right."

"Let's see if it's worth the five hundred dollars we paid for it."

Susan excused herself to the outer office while the men went to work. She sat down at her desk and began to sort through the pile of newspapers. The lead story of the first paper was *Seagulls Triumph Over Rosemont.* Skimming the story, Susan learned that the village men's softball team had beaten arch rival Rosemont in the district finals, assuring them a berth in the state playoffs to be held July thirtieth. That would have been over a month ago. Idly Susan wondered if the Seagulls had taken the state championship.

Other stories that week concerned a garage fire caused by careless storage of gasoline and an announcement by the Gull Harbor Public Library that it was sponsoring a summer vacation readathon.

From the other room she heard a couple of clanks and a thud, then the low drone of a motor. It appeared the beast was operable again.

Flipping to the inside pages, Susan

noted the usual engagement and wedding announcements, several with pictures of smiling couples. There was a small classified section, a syndicated column on boating, and another column with the header "Closet Poet."

Intrigued, Susan read the featured poem, "Mist," by K. Garnett. She'd always enjoyed poetry, though she was no expert on the subject. "Mist" was a very lovely poem, she found. The words evoked soft images of a misty shore and the meter was good.

Susan deduced the column must also be syndicated. She wondered if Paul cared for poetry himself or had bowed to the wishes of his subscribers, perhaps certain female members of a local poetry society. The idea that conjured up made her smile.

Laying aside the paper, she picked up the next one on the stack. Instantly her smile faded, her eyes riveted to the bold headline on the first page: *No Progress in the Amy Lambert Case.* A shiver ran up Susan's spine.

The article was short, just two columns, but there was a photograph beside the article. An angelic-looking child with blond hair stared out at her, smiling. It was Amy Lambert.

Joey Peterson had been blond. And in the photos Stephanie had shown her, he had always been smiling. "A trusting child," Stephanie had said, voice trembling. Had Amy Lambert been trusting?

At the sound of Paul's voice, Susan let out a little gasp. Hastily she shoved the paper under the others in the stack.

Paul was talking to Steven, but they had emerged from the back room and were coming her way. The two men stopped by her desk. After bidding her good-bye, Steven went out the front door of the office.

Susan took a deep breath before looking at Paul. She prayed he wouldn't detect her unease.

He met her eyes, unblinking. "Susan?" he said quizzically.

She almost told him what was troubling her, but she sensed it wasn't the time nor the place. She promised herself she would talk to him soon, once she'd had a chance to go over the other papers and see what further articles she might find on Amy. "I heard the beast rumble to life," she said, offering a shaky smile.

"Yes." Paul spread his palms on her desk, bending close to her.

She thought she could feel his warm

breath on her face. His gaze was drawn to her lips and she felt a different sort of unease. Dropping her eyes to study her desk, she heard him say, "It's closing time, Susan."

Peering up from lowered lashes, she watched Paul go to the door and reverse the sign that hung there. He didn't return to her desk and she got up, gathering the copies of the *Beacon* in her arms.

He held the door open for her. "I had a great time the other day, showing you the local sights," he said as she stood in front of him.

Susan realized she hadn't even thanked him properly. "I appreciate you taking the time to do that, Paul. I enjoyed it . . . a lot." Pausing, she added, "I'll see you Friday."

Susan stepped outside, but before Paul could shut the door, she asked, "Can you tell me what my first assignment will be?"

His mouth curved up a little. "One of two rallies. The developer's or the environmentalists'."

Susan regarded him. "The fight over Barr Estuary."

"That's right."

"I'm looking forward to it, then." She was being sincere, though she secretly hoped she would get to cover the environmentalists' meeting. "I hope the rallies don't get rained out."

Paul laughed. "I thought you said you love rain."

"I do," she retorted, her lips pouting slightly. "But I wonder about the developer."

"You've got a point," Paul acknowledged. He leaned against the door frame, crossing his arms. "But I guarantee it won't stop the Gull Harbor Conservation Society. The environmentalists," he added.

"Good. See you Friday, Paul." Susan tore herself away from the sincere gaze he'd set upon her and walked resolutely to her car.

Pulling away from the curb, she headed down Main Street. As she came to Bears' Tea Party, Susan slowed the Subaru, debating whether to stop and see Anna. But the place looked dark and she saw the CLOSED sign hanging in the window. Still, the stuffed animals loyally kept their sentry posts and she imagined Anna was there, conversing with the large white bear sporting the red tie around its neck. The fanciful thought evoked in Susan that same odd mingling of amusement and melancholy she'd felt before.

Chapter Four

The next morning Susan went in search of a grocery store. She found one just off Main Street. It was called Glendig's Market, and though it was small, Susan discovered it had an excellent produce section and an old-fashioned butcher counter where meats were custom-cut.

She spent more time in the market and bought more than she'd intended to. When she got back to the cottage and unpacked her groceries, she guessed she wouldn't have to shop again for a couple of weeks.

Looking out the window, Susan saw that the sky, which had been overcast earlier, had cleared. It should be a perfect afternoon for a trip to Barr Estuary.

She gathered her camera equipment and notebook, packed a few wedges of Brie cheese and some fruit in a bag, then stuffed her swamp waders and a jacket into her knapsack.

From her deck, she scanned the bright expanse of water. Sunlight was scattered on the surface like so many diamonds. Not far out, a sloop's mainsail billowed tall and full against the tranquil background of blue sky and sea.

Before she started for the marina, Susan paused, peering in the direction of Rodney's cottage. She wondered what it looked like behind its cover of trees. For a moment she debated whether to check it out. She could casually stroll down the beach and happen by the back of his home.

"Uh-uh, another time," she muttered to herself, turning the other way. She was curious about Rodney's cottage and his yacht, but not that much.

The estuary was everything Susan had anticipated, and she soon filled a number of pages in her notebook. But she found she wasn't enjoying the refuge nearly as much as she had in Paul's company.

She'd never minded poking around swampy places by herself. Complete solitude was her choice for doing research. But from the short afternoon she'd spent with Paul, she had learned his company wasn't intrusive nor distracting — except, she reminded herself, for those times when his eyes had captured hers, threatening to upset any pretense at studiousness.

So she was better off by herself, after all. Not a convincing argument, she concluded, giggling as she put on her waders and began to walk carefully along a marshy area near where the *Anne Marie* was anchored.

Susan used up two rolls of film and was starting on a third when she decided she'd better head back to the marina.

The sea was dead calm and she had to resort to using the motor on her small craft. Few other boats shared the water with her. Maybe that was why she didn't notice the ketch at first.

She had no idea from which direction it had come. She only realized that it seemed to be circling her. Not too closely, not at first. But with each pass — and by this time she knew the ketch was purposely circling the *Anne Marie* — it drew nearer. She saw three men on board. They looked young, maybe in their thirties. They whistled and waved at her.

Guys out for a good time, trying to scare her, Susan told herself. Her hands gripped the tiller of the *Anne Marie* more tightly. She was determined not to give them the satisfaction of thinking they'd rattled her.

"Hey, babe, I'm in love!"

The ketch had drawn very close alongside. The man who'd called to her held up a can. Probably a beer can, Susan thought grimly. Were the men drunk?

She made a sharp left turn away from the ketch, but not before she caught the name written in bold black letters on the boat's bow. *Mach III*. It figured.

Looking straight ahead, Susan kept the *Anne Marie* on course for the marina. The *Mach III* made two more passes, then suddenly left, veering off to the north. Maybe it was because the dock was in sight.

After tethering the *Anne Marie*, Susan went into the marina, spotting Sam behind the lunch counter. She hoped she wouldn't appear foolish telling him about the incident.

As casually as she could, she asked him whether a ketch called *Mach III* was berthed at his dock.

Sam gazed at her for a long moment as he wiped the counter with a towel. "No boat by that name moored here." He tossed the towel aside. "Why?"

Susan shrugged. "Nothing, really. Just that a boatload of guys chased me. They made a nuisance of themselves for a while. Circling close, waving and yelling. That sort of thing."

Sam's eyes narrowed. "Did they threaten you?"

Susan's heartbeat quickened again. "No." She licked her lips. "I . . . did feel a bit uneasy." She'd always been one to understate the facts.

Sam scowled. "Listen, Susan, if that ever happens again, I'll take care of it. Their boat might not be docked here, but I can see that they learn a lesson or two."

Susan got the impression that he *could* take care of the problem, never mind that he might be twice as old and not half as husky as the men. "Thanks, Sam." She smiled up at him.

Sam gave her a wink. She started to leave, but he called her back. "Just a minute, Susan." He handed her a wrapped package. "This one's on the house."

An inviting odor met her nose. "Some of the best fish and chips I've eaten," she remarked as she turned away. She was glad she'd told him about the incident. And she promised herself she wouldn't anticipate any future encounters with the ungentlemanly crew of the *Mach III*.

By Thursday, a storm had come in, heavy clouds hovering low over the ocean. If it had been winter, the gale might have been called a nor'easter. As it was, the wind blew fiercely, hurling the rain in sheets against the windows of the cottage.

Despite her love of inclement weather, Susan decided it was a good day to stay in. The baseboard heaters in the cottage made popping and sizzling noises when she turned up the thermostat. A fire would have been cozier and there was a stone fireplace in one corner of the living room, but no wood. She reminded herself to pick up a cord or two when she went into town the next day.

After making a cup of peppermint tea, she curled up on the sofa and picked a newspaper from the stack Paul had given her. She shoved aside thoughts of the issue on the bottom of the pile, the one with the article about Amy.

Her brief examination of the *Beacon* on Tuesday had convinced her the paper was of high quality, both in content and general layout. Paul was a fine newspaperman.

She skimmed through most of the issues, but always checked out the "Closet Poet" column. Most of the poems bore the name K. Garnett; they were all good, many of them about the sea. A couple of the columns had poems by guest poets. No doubt they were members of the Gull Harbor

Poetry Society, as Susan had dubbed it in her mind.

She smiled at the thought, but grew sober when she realized she'd come to the bottom of the pile of papers. Her hand rested on the issue with the article about Amy.

Susan wanted to forget that article. She couldn't. Taking the paper in her hands, she read the report. It only revealed that no new leads had turned up in the case. Robert Osborn, the detective on the case, said that there still was no evidence of foul play, but that Amy's father, Sean Lambert, was the prime suspect in the presumed kidnapping.

Farther down the column, Glen Glendig, sheriff of Gull Harbor, commented that he was pleased with the efforts of Detective Osborn, that everything possible had been done to find Amy. "It's my belief that if Sean Lambert is found, the case will be resolved," the sheriff opined. He went on to reveal that an all-points bulletin had been issued with no success to date. He speculated that father and daughter had fled to Canada.

Susan slowly lowered the paper. Rain pounded on the roof. Did Amy like rain? Was she someplace safe and warm? Or was she. . . .

"Don't!" The self-imposed reprimand echoed in the insistent beat of the rain. Susan got up abruptly from the sofa and paced into the kitchen over to the small window above the sink. Rivulets of water snaked down the pane, distorting the view of the turbulent gray ocean. Darkness had descended like a bleak shroud, though it was only mid afternoon.

She felt angry, like the clouds that had pressed in from the sea. Who was she angry at? The good sheriff? Detective Osborn? Or nameless others who might have worked, might still be working, on the case?

Susan knew it was ridiculous to blame the authorities for not finding the child. But she'd read a certain smugness into the sheriff's words, as though he and his detective had dismissed all other possibilities except parental abduction.

Remembering the grocery where she'd shopped the day before, Susan wondered if the sheriff owned it. Or one of his relatives. Was Gull Harbor the kind of town where a certain family seemed to dominate the politics and business aspects of the community?

If the Glendig name meant power in Gull Harbor, Paul would know. Paul isn't a

Glendig, Susan thought with a smile. *Nor is Rodney*, a small voice reminded her. She wondered how much interest Rodney took in village affairs. If the rather nonchalant way he'd told her about Amy's kidnapping was any indication, it was unlikely he took any interest at all.

On the other hand, wasn't she over-reacting, as though she were about to launch a crusade to solve the kidnapping? But the Peterson case had taught her too much and left her haunted by doubt. It had sensitized her beyond reason to every other missing child case she heard about.

Though she had no appetite, she put together a sandwich. Absently she cut a roll in two and piled slices of roast beef and cheese on one half. She tore off a large leaf from the head of lettuce she'd thought looked so fine on display at Glendig's Market and cut a plump tomato into thick slices.

When the sandwich was assembled, Susan had to laugh despite herself. The unwieldly creation resembled the trade-mark of a certain famous cartoon char-acter.

She managed to eat half of it, then wrapped the other half to put in the refrigerator. She could take it along for lunch the next day.

Trying to set her mind on her prospective assignment for the *Beacon*, Susan took a shower and washed her hair. The distraction helped, and after her shower, she went through her closet to choose what she would wear to work the next day. She pulled out a rose-colored skirt and matching blouse. The outfit always drew compliments, though the effect might be lost if she had to cover it with her trench coat.

But she wouldn't have to wear her trench coat indoors at the office. The idea made her smile, but she had to ask herself who she was trying to impress. It wouldn't be a certain editor, would it?

"I thought about you yesterday."

The editor in question gave Susan an innocent smile, though the confession seemed to hold interesting possibilities.

"Is that so?" she asked just as innocently, turning to hang up her coat. Her mind registered that Paul looked exceptionally good in the pale yellow shirt and complementary striped tie he was sporting.

"I was covering a football game," he went on. "The Gull Harbor High versus the Pitston Pirates."

She tossed him a curious glance. "Let me guess. The final score was thirty to zip. In favor of the Seagulls, of course."

"Nope." He smiled broadly. "*Fifty* to zip."

Susan passed a hand across her eyes. "Spare me the gruesome details."

"But that's not why I thought of you, Susan."

"No?" She lowered her hand.

He shook his head. "It was raining. Not just *raining*," he corrected, "a no-holds-barred, drenching downpour. I got soaked."

"But you were prepared for the weather, weren't you?" His nod was affirmative. "What about the poor players, not to mention the fans? Think of the fans. I'll bet the stadium doesn't even have a roof."

"Fans? What are they? The stadium, as you optimistically called twenty rows of bleachers, was empty."

"Oh. Well, I assume you knew the hazards of this job when you took it. You didn't expect to cover only indoor events, did you? Or . . . was that why you hired me? To brave the elements so you won't have to?" Had she gone too far in her teasing? One glance at his face told her she hadn't, that he was enjoying their banter as much as she was.

"I just thought," he began, fingering the knot in his tie, "that you would have been far more suited for the assignment, what with your love of rain and your fine trench coat."

But he wasn't looking at the trench coat. His gaze washed over her appreciatively.

Averting her eyes, Susan gazed out the window. It was still raining; maybe not a drenching downpour, but close. "I guess I'll get my chance today," she said, reminding herself she shouldn't flirt with her boss. But what should she do when her boss was the one doing the flirting?

"We'll *both* get our chance." He seemed to remember there was work to be done. Going over to his desk, he returned with a sheet of paper. "Actually, I've got two assignments for you. You'll be covering the Conservation Society's rally at Barr Estuary this afternoon. It starts at two." He peered at her over the rim of his glasses. They'd slipped down again. Pushing them up, he muttered, "I've got to get these things fixed."

Susan speculated with amusement that he'd probably neglected getting the glasses tightened for a very long time. "Sounds good. I mean, the part about covering the environmentalists' rally." Her flustered comment drew a chuckle from Paul. "What's my other assignment?" she asked a bit meekly.

"A tea on Sunday afternoon. It's considered one of Gull Harbor's social events of the year, at least for the ladies of the town." He paused, adding, "The tea is held at Miss Ruth Westman's home. The address and other instructions are on the sheet. I also drew a map of the route to the estuary. I don't suppose you'll be going by boat today."

Susan laughed. "I hadn't planned on that mode of transportation. Do you want pictures of both the rally and the tea?"

"Don't bother this afternoon, but yes, be sure to take plenty of photos of the ladies attending the tea. They like to see themselves on the, ah, society page of the paper."

Covering the event sounded like fun to Susan. "What about a camera? Should I use my own?" He hadn't mentioned *how* she was to take the photos.

"I'm sorry, Susan. I should have told you that we have a camera in the office. But if you'd be more comfortable using your own equipment, I can reimburse you for the cost of the film. There's a closet-size darkroom in back." Paul perched himself on a corner of her desk. "You're welcome to sit down, you know."

She hadn't realized she was still standing. "That's okay. I'm comfortable." Not entirely, she realized. His close proximity to her had a definite unnerving effect. Checking her watch, she saw it was eleven-thirty.

"Time for lunch already?"

Susan's face grew warm. "Not yet."

"You can leave now, if you like." Paul got up and stretched his arms above his head.

For a moment, she thought he was going to invite her to lunch, but he didn't. Instead, he went over and retrieved her coat. "Don't forget this." He grinned.

She took the coat from him. "Should I turn in my report on the rally today?"

"No." He began to walk her to the door. "You'll need to have both stories ready by nine o'clock on Sunday night. We print early Monday. Usually, that is."

She suspected the "usually" depended on whether the beast was up for printing.

"Any other questions?"

The soft way he said it disarmed her. There was a question she'd like to ask. But it was hardly proper to query your boss about personal matters. Even if his eyes,

84

those eyes you could get lost in, were regarding you with barely disguised interest.

Shaking her head, Susan turned and went out the door to her car. She ate the leftover half of the roast beef sandwich as she slowly drove down Main Street. There was some time to kill before heading for the estuary, so she decided to stop in at Bears' Tea Party.

The OPEN sign was posted today and the door was even ajar a little, despite the rain.

"Hello, Susan dear."

The greeting rang out as soon as Susan stepped inside the shop. "Anna." She smiled at the older woman. "I told you I'd be back soon."

"And here you are." Anna's face wore a pleased expression.

Susan noted that the elderly proprietor appeared relaxed. There was no sign of the former distress caused by the gruff customer.

"Did you get the reporter job, dear?"

"Yes."

Anna's smile widened. "I just knew you would. Isn't that Paul Stuart a lovely man? And, you know, he's unattached."

Susan smiled to herself at the older woman's repetition of Paul's marital status.

But she wasn't about to confide her feelings on the matter. "He's very nice," she replied, borrowing Anna's former compliment.

"I'm sure he was equally impressed with you, dear."

Now what did Anna mean by that? Susan decided it was time to change the subject. "I thought I might see about getting a bear or two for my cottage."

"Oh, any of them would be quite pleased for you to adopt them. You did meet Benjamin and Mathilde, didn't you?" Anna took hold of Susan's hand.

"Gertrude and Sylvester too." Susan found herself being led into the alcove.

"They had a lively discussion about you after you left the other day."

"They did?" Susan didn't mean to sound startled.

"Rest assured all of it was good. They're very fond of you, Susan."

"I. . . . I'm fond of them too, Anna." She wondered just how much make-believe blurred with reality in Anna's mind.

"They're both handsome couples, don't you think?" Anna patted Sylvester's head.

"Yes, extremely handsome."

Anna looked up at Susan. A pained expression etched her face. "It's so tragic."

Her voice trembled.

"What?" Susan automatically reached out to touch Anna's arm.

"About Benjamin and Mathilde." Anna sadly shook her head. "I'm afraid their family no longer wanted them."

"What?" Susan cleared her throat. Carefully she asked, "Why wouldn't they want Benjamin and Mathilde?"

"Seth and Sara brought them in to me. Seth and Sara are twins." Anna smiled briefly, but the smile soon faded. "Sara said they were too old for teddy bears now. They had other toys to play with. Can you imagine such a thing?" Anna looked at Susan, incredulous.

Before Susan could respond, Anna continued, "Poor little dears. They've been with me ever since. I don't suppose I could ever give them up. I do think the special clothes I made for them cheered them a bit." Anna's voice sounded hopeful.

"The outfits are very beautiful. I'm sure they're quite happy." Susan had the urge to hug Anna, but she refrained. Anna was vulnerable, all right, perhaps more than she'd first thought. She did believe the bears were alive and had feelings like people. What other fantasies might the older woman harbor?

"Come, I want you to meet some of the others who are waiting for a good home."

Susan followed Anna back into the main room of the shop. "What about that one, Anna?" She pointed to a white bear in the window.

Anna lowered her eyes and clucked softly under her breath. "I'm terribly sorry, Susan. Christopher's spoken for."

"I'm sorry too." Just then Susan realized he would have been perfect for that empty spot by the fireplace.

"But let me introduce you to Deborah and Chesterfield."

Many more introductions later, Susan saw that the time was slipping away. If she wanted to get to Barr Estuary to cover the rally, she'd have to go. "I just don't know, Anna. Every bear is precious. I don't want to make a hasty decision."

Anna's eyes lit up. "Why don't you take them all?"

Susan laughed, then wondered if Anna was really joking. "I can't promise to do that, but I want at least two. I'm afraid that I need to be on my way. Paul gave me my first assignment. I'm covering a rally at Barr Estuary."

"My, he's making you go out in all this rain." Anna frowned disapprovingly.

"Honestly, I don't mind. You might remember that I said I enjoy rain."

"Oh well, then I can forgive him, dear." Anna patted Susan's hand.

"I'll see you again soon, Anna."

"Take care, Susan."

Just as Susan was about to open the door to leave, a tall, elegantly dressed woman came in, sweeping by her to Anna.

"Ruth, dear!" Anna exclaimed.

"Anna, how are you?" the woman asked.

Susan watched Anna and Ruth embrace. Somehow she knew this must be Ruth Westman, who was hostessing the tea on Sunday. Quietly she left the shop while Anna's attention was diverted. But when she paused on the sidewalk and looked back, she saw Anna standing by the window, waving at her. She waved in turn, glad that at least for today Anna had someone to talk to besides her bears.

Chapter Five

"The people of Gull Harbor cannot tolerate the spoiling of this sanctuary. We *will* triumph over the greedy plans of Harlan Brown, a proven enemy of this fair refuge. Barr Estuary must be preserved not only for ourselves but for our children and grandchildren and all generations to come!"

Thornton Pierce, president of the Gull Harbor Conservation Society, put down the bullhorn he'd been speaking through and raised his arms in a victory sign.

The considerable crowd that had gathered roared their approval and support.

Susan hurried to finish writing her notes. Despite the unrelenting downpour, the rally had lasted more than an hour and the society members showed unflagging optimism. She wished she could say the same for herself. Holding her umbrella between her arm and rib cage while trying to scribble notes had caused her hand to cramp. And she was beginning to see why Paul had been so unenthusiastic about covering the football game in the rain.

Fishing in her tote bag for a new pen, she started to make her way over to Thornton Pierce. She wanted to ask him a few questions.

She shifted her umbrella for a better view through the crowd and felt the frame bump against something.

"Watch it, lady."

Even before she turned, Susan knew the harsh voice. She recognized the combat boots too. They were the first thing she saw as she whirled around. Peering out from underneath her umbrella, she faced the man who had put a look of fear in Anna Winston's eyes.

He was dressed in the same black slicker, the hood of it now drawn over his head. Only his features and unkempt beard were visible. His eyes glowered at her, his lips curled into a snarl.

"I'm sorry," Susan mumbled, peeved that he should intimidate her.

"Susan." Someone touched her arm and she looked abruptly in the other direction.

"Paul." She couldn't have been more glad to see him — or more surprised.

Paul stared at her curiously. Then his gaze shifted to the man behind her. "Is there a problem, Travers?" he said shortly.

The name cut through Susan like a knife. The man she had bumped was Daryl Travers. The man who'd paid a surly visit to Bears' Tea Party had been Daryl Travers.

Tension was suddenly thick in the air. She could feel it as her eyes traveled from Paul to Travers and back again. She sensed the animosity between the two men.

Finally Travers muttered something Susan couldn't hear, but it sounded more like a grunt than words. Then he turned on his heel and strode off.

"Are you all right?"

Paul regarded her with undisguised concern. "I'm fine," Susan said too quickly. She busied herself by stuffing her notepad and pen into her bag. "So that was the owner of Rocky Pointe Lighthouse."

"Very unfortunately."

She gave Paul a little smile. He was wearing a beige trench coat.

"The rain's stopped," he offered.

Lowering her umbrella, she saw that it had. Paul's hair was slightly wet, meaning he'd caught at least some of the downpour. The dampness darkened the wavy strands, enhancing their appeal in a most wonderful way, she noticed. "That isn't the first time I've seen Daryl Travers."

Paul took hold of her elbow briefly and began to guide her through the disbanding crowd. "No?"

Susan glanced back at Paul, explaining, "He came into Bears' Tea Party my first day in town. I'd gone there for a cup of tea and met Anna Winston. She's very sweet."

"Anna Winston's a wonderful woman." Paul's words conveyed warmth. "Too bad she's Travers's neighbor."

"His neighbor?"

Paul indicated a wooden sidewalk to their left, marked Spruce Trail. They began to walk that way. "Anna's property shares a common boundary with his. But as you were saying about Travers and Bears' Tea Party. . . ."

"I was sitting in the alcove," she continued, "having tea and a turnover, when he came marching in. I noticed him right away. He looked out of place there."

"Like the proverbial bull in the china shop."

Susan laughed. "Exactly." She paused, observing the view. Tall grass dominated the mainly marshy area. Small backwater ponds were visible through the undergrowth. "He talked with Anna, or rather intimidated her, though I couldn't hear their conversation."

"Do you think Travers threatened her in some way?" Paul's eyes narrowed, his fingers curving around a handrail.

Susan shrugged. "I don't know, but she gave him some sort of package. I did hear her say 'it's all there,' whatever that meant. You don't suppose he bought a set of teddy bears or miniature china service, do you?" She wanted to lighten the mood, but Paul didn't smile.

"For his mother, perhaps. As I understand it, she's a collector of antiques. So he could have been picking up a purchase for her."

"And maybe Anna had gotten the order wrong or something."

"Maybe."

They resumed their stroll. Somewhere, from one of the taller trees, came the call of a loon. "But Travers was here today. He must be in favor of saving the estuary," she said.

Paul laughed this time. "Daryl Travers's main concern is to look out for himself. His property begins at the northern boundary of the estuary. If Harlan Brown comes in and builds an apartment complex, a shopping center and traffic jams are sure to follow. And there goes Daryl Travers's privacy."

94

"I see what you mean." Susan turned and drank in the peaceful scene. Cord grass swayed gracefully in the breeze, anchored by the dunes. "This is a beautiful place. I can't fault Travers for wanting to save it."

"I suppose not."

The reply was hardly charitable, but Susan hadn't expected it to be. Travers was a frightening man, though bumping into him didn't make her any less determined to visit the tide pools below his lighthouse. She'd just have to be extra cautious.

"Would you like to sit down? The bench might be a little wet, but . . ."

Paul's invitation drew Susan from her introspection. There was a bench at the side of the walkway. "I don't mind the wetness," she said, promptly settling herself down beside him. She took in the serene setting. "I can see why you come here often. But why did you come here *today*?" Just now it had occurred to her to ask that question.

His eyes twinkled, a deeper hue at that moment than the sky on a cloudless afternoon. "Was I checking up on you? Isn't that what you mean?"

Susan felt herself blush. He knew just

what to say to fluster her. "Now that you mention it, yes."

Paul chuckled, unbuttoning his coat as he leaned back against the bench. "Harlan Brown didn't show for his rally, only a few of his supporters. It must have taken me ten minutes to interview them."

"So you thought you'd head for where the action was."

"I told you the environmentalists wouldn't stop for rain." He fiddled with the last button on his coat. "I have to confess I wanted to see how you fared in the downpour."

"I didn't melt." The saucy remark drew the desired response.

Amusement crinkled the corners of his eyes. Bending close to her, he said, "No. I'd say you survived . . . admirably." His gaze held hers. "I saw from your application you live out on Quay Road," he said, switching the subject.

With the mention of her cottage came a swift change in Susan's mood. "That's right," she said, drawing a deep breath. There seemed no better time to ask him about Amy. "I learned something about my cottage recently."

"What's that?"

"I met an old classmate of mine on the

beach. His name is Rodney Silvers. Maybe you know him."

Paul's eyebrows arched. "Not well." The short reply gave Susan the notion he wouldn't care to know Rodney better.

"Anyway, he told me that a woman named Chris Lambert and her daughter, Amy, lived in the cottage before me. He said that Amy went out to play one day and disappeared."

Paul's eyes took on an unfocused look. "Yes. She disappeared without a trace, as the saying goes."

"Paul, there was an article in one of the issues of the *Beacon* that you gave me." She couldn't keep a note of urgency from her voice. Pressing on, she said, "The article quoted the sheriff and a detective named Osborn. They believed Amy was abducted by her father. They seemed so sure of that."

Paul's face wore a grim expression. "You're right. That's what the authorities conjecture."

Touching his sleeve, Susan asked, "Is it what you think? You must have followed the case closely."

"Very closely. But does it matter what I think?" His words held a certain irony.

"To me it does," she replied gently.

"Because you reported on a similar case," he said just as gently. "Because you got emotionally involved."

"It was impossible not to. I wasn't a seasoned reporter then."

He glanced skeptically at her. "And you believe seasoned reporters never cross that line of objectivity?"

He seemed to think she was naïve, and it rankled her. But only for a moment. She knew he must be talking about himself. And suddenly she had to know the reason why he had left Detroit to run a small-town newspaper — if he was willing to tell her. Another time she would be sure to pursue the subject of Amy Lambert's disappearance.

"Are you thinking about the case?" he prompted. "Does it bother you to live in the cottage?"

"Yes . . . a little," she admitted. "But I'm also thinking about you." He looked mildly surprised, yet glad. "I can tell you enjoy Gull Harbor, Paul, and you do a super job with the paper. You said you needed a major change. Why was that? What prompted you to leave Detroit and the *Free Press*?"

Paul's expression turned serious; he averted his eyes. Several moments passed while he seemed to search for a reply.

Susan was almost ready to apologize, to fill the void with some inane comment, when he cleared his throat. Turning to her, he said, "Something happened after I moved back to Detroit, Susan. Something terrible." His eyes probed hers, as dark and brooding now as a sky turned stormy.

"I'm sorry," she whispered, meaning she was sorry both for whatever caused that look of pain and for being nosey.

He locked his hands together in front of him. "It's all right. Actually, I think I wanted you to ask." His mouth curved in a brief smile, no doubt at the ambiguity of his words. "I'd been with the *Free Press* for a couple of years when I met someone. Her name was Andrea Wellsley, and she was a secretary at a company where a friend of mine worked. He introduced us." Paul paused. "I'd never been serious about anyone before."

"But you were about Andrea," Susan offered quietly.

"We started dating, just occasionally at first. It wasn't long before we were beginning to get involved, to talk about a future together."

"What happened?" Susan thought she was prepared for Paul's reply.

But he slumped visibly, head bowed, as though all the energy and animation that were characteristic of him had suddenly vanished. "She . . . Andrea was murdered."

The words hit Susan with the force of a physical blow. She'd been expecting him to say he and Andrea had argued and broken up, or even that Andrea had left him for someone else. She drew a sharp breath that made her chest ache. "Murdered? How?" In the charged air between them, the agony Paul must have endured was like a palpable thing to her.

"Andrea was coming home from work that day, as usual. She always walked. Her apartment building was only a couple of blocks away from the C. T. Best Building. That was the company she worked for." He glanced at Susan. His expression conveyed how difficult the retelling was for him. "It was winter, already dark at six o'clock in the evening. It had snowed. Two young thugs attacked her. Looking for drug money, according to the officer who got there too late." Paul's voice was bitter. "They shot Andrea. She died instantly, I was told."

Automatically Susan reached for his hand. "No." The whispered word seemed so inadequate, so did those that followed.

"I'm so sorry, Paul." Sorry for the nightmarish tragedy he'd endured. Sorry that she'd ever asked why he left Detroit for Gull Harbor.

"I am too," he told her, turning her hand to cover it with his. "I went through all the stages of grief. Denial, anger, the feeling of total helplessness. I finally joined a support group. After awhile, I thought I was ready to experience the last stage of the grieving process, to accept what I couldn't change."

"But you still didn't stay in the city after that."

His eyes met hers. "I did stay for another year and a half. I threw myself into my job. I didn't date, had no social life to speak of. That's why I was up for the promotion." His mouth curved again in a sad smile. "Diligence has its rewards, I guess."

"I suppose it does."

He continued. "I was on the fast track, about to have the title of assistant news editor bestowed on me. Not so shabby for a twenty-seven-year-old hack reporter."

That provoked a little smile from her. "Not shabby at all. Yet a title wasn't important to you, was it?"

He leaned nearer. His softly expelled breath warmed her face. "I've got a title now, Susan, and more of a reason to be a workaholic than ever. The change, the move to Gull Harbor, has generally been good for me, but . . ."

Paul looked suddenly doubtful. "But?" Susan coaxed. A small quiver of anticipation began deep inside her. Anticipation of *what?*

"It wasn't until I came out here that I went through that final stage I was telling you about."

"Acceptance," she said gently. Somewhere in the background a goshawk gave a muted cry.

"Yes, and then I began to see that as much as I enjoy my work, and I do enjoy the newspaper business," he emphasized, "I needed a life outside of the office. It isn't wrong to want that."

"Not wrong at all," Susan was quick to say. Though he had turned partially away from her, she noticed the tension in his face had begun to ease, the muscles of his neck and jaw relaxing slightly.

"It was one of the things we hashed over a lot in the support group back in Detroit. Everyone there had been through pretty much the same kind of experience I'd had. I learned the hardest feeling to overcome is guilt, thinking that it's wrong to want happiness again when someone you love and care about so much is gone." He raked a hand through his hair. "I guess it just took me longer than most people to work it out."

Susan imagined he was being too hard on himself. She also believed she understood why he had been so adamantly opposed to her visiting the tide pools below Travers's property. The brutal murder of the woman he'd loved had sensitized Paul to see danger in circumstances where another person might be apt to shrug it off. "What you've felt is only normal," she said at last.

He gave her a grateful glance. "I did start to date again after I moved here, but only casually." He removed his glasses. Capturing her eyes with his, he said, "I don't know how to tell you . . . the right words. Maybe I shouldn't say it at all." His unease was obvious, as was the pleading look he gave her.

"Just try," she urged, not sure what he wanted to tell her now, not sure it was something she wanted to hear. At the moment, she only longed to offer sympathy as best she could — and only knew that with the barrier of his glasses gone, she was fast becoming lost in his eyes.

"Since Andrea, I didn't think I . . ." He

stopped short, then seemed to gather his courage. "I didn't believe I'd ever meet another woman I could feel that way about again. That is, until you."

"Until me?" Susan echoed, not trusting that she had heard him right.

He shook his head, but his hand held hers more tightly and he laid his glasses aside on the bench. "I know it shouldn't be like this. You just came to town. You were looking for part-time work. I was looking to hire a reporter. Our relationship should be strictly business. Right, Susan?"

His eyes lowered to study her lips, and for all his sincerity, he couldn't hide his true feelings. Wasn't that what she wanted? To know that he'd apparently been attracted to her from the first, the same way she had been to him? Yet a small doubt tried to creep in and tell her that maybe in some unconscious way she reminded him of Andrea. Had Andrea been slender? Had her hair been dark and curly? Her eyes brown? Forcing the troubling notion aside, Susan asked, "Is this what you call strictly business, Paul?"

"No, not strictly. . . ." The words were cut off as he brought his mouth to hers, accepting her silent invitation.

There was a hesitation in the kiss, as

though he was still not sure it was the proper thing to do. She let him know it was by wrapping her arms around his neck. He responded, pulling her closer.

The kiss was gentle, sweet, and Susan sensed that Paul was drawing comfort from the tender press of her lips against his. Her fingers stroked the nape of his neck. If it was comfort he wanted and needed, she would gladly give it.

When they drew apart, his arms still held her, one hand buried in the thick curls of her hair. "Listen," he whispered.

She listened. There was the muted croaking of a bullfrog from his hidden pond. The same clear cry of the hawk she'd heard before, nearer now. "I hear," she whispered back.

"Smell the air," Paul invited, pressing his nose against her cheek.

She sniffed. "It smells crisp and clean."

"Fall is coming," he added, leaning back a bit to observe her.

Susan saw that the sadness was gone from his eyes. She felt contentment in that. In fact, she felt so contented that she didn't care if he held her to him forever. "I can see why you come to the estuary often," she said finally. "But when I came here alone, the place didn't seem half as enchanting as it does now."

Paul's cheeks took on a ruddy hue that was most becoming. He averted his eyes, checking his watch.

The act triggered a response in Susan, remembrance of an obligation she'd made and entirely forgotten in Paul's company. "Oh, no! What time is it?" The blurted words drew a startled look from Paul.

"Nearly five. Why? I was just about to ask if you'd like to have dinner some —"

"I have to go," she interrupted, reaching for her tote bag. Flustered, she stole a glance at Paul. "I'm sorry. I've got an engagement this evening."

"A date," he confirmed.

Susan's cheeks warmed. She squirmed uncomfortably, the cozy mood of only moments before gone. "Yes."

Paul swiftly released her and rose from the bench. "With Rodney Silvers," he guessed, his voice flat.

"Well, yes," she admitted. She didn't see Paul's reaction. His back was to her; he was picking up his glasses. She wanted to say that she had no interest at all in going out with Rodney, wanted to tell him she would forget the date and go to dinner with him. She'd make up a reason to tell Rodney later.

But she couldn't. And what would Paul think of her if she did? She'd never had any respect for those who broke their promises and made up excuses. She wouldn't expect any less from Paul. So she said nothing, all the while longing for him to hold her again, if just for a second.

He didn't, and their return to the parking area where they'd left their cars was peppered with awkward silences. Susan couldn't begin to guess what was going through Paul's mind. Maybe he felt foolish for opening up to her and letting her know in such an obvious way that he cared for her. Or maybe he was sensitive to her feelings of embarrassment over the circumstances that had abruptly ended their time together.

Whatever it was, he wasn't opening up to her now. Nor could she expect him to.

They stopped by her car. Someone had to end the silence. "Will I see you on Sunday evening then, Paul?" She had her fingers crossed inside the pockets of her coat.

He looked confused for a second. "Oh. Sunday. You'll be at the office."

"You said I needed to have my stories ready for printing by nine."

He smiled a little, drawing himself up

straight as he shoved his hands into his coat pockets. "Yes, I'll be there."

"Okay. See you," she said softly, resisting the overwhelming urge to fling her arms around him and kiss him until he had no question about her feelings for him.

He backed away from her, then turned and walked quickly to his car.

Even though it would set her even further behind in getting ready for her date, Susan stood and watched until Paul got into the small station wagon and pulled out of the parking area.

Chapter Six

"Are you having a good time, Susan?"

Rodney's voice was low, persuasive. His arm came up to rest on the back of the plush booth where Susan was seated beside him.

How should she answer his question? "The band's great." Susan dropped her eyes to study her glass of Chablis. "And the atmosphere's definitely tony."

When she glanced up, she wasn't surprised to see a look of displeasure on Rodney's face. He had wined her and dined her. He had danced with her — and he was a very good dancer. He'd spent a lot of money on her.

Besides, hadn't every other woman in the place tossed envious glances her way? Hadn't those same women eyed Rodney with open interest? He couldn't be oblivious to the attention he'd been receiving. No wonder her evasive reply didn't agree with him.

But it seemed he wasn't giving up. He

flashed her a cocky grin, then confided softly, "I bring all my dates here. You're not the first, you know."

Maybe he meant to make her jealous with the flippant remark. Or he might be trying to humor her.

Susan forced a little laugh. "I think I saw some of them tonight, Rodney." She took a careful sip of her Chablis.

The grin widened. "I'm sure of it," he retorted, his arm slipping from the back of the booth to come around her waist. He pulled her close in a smooth move, whispering, "But none of them are as beautiful as you."

Instinctively she wanted to draw away. Was she crazy? Here she was with Mr. Charm and all she could think about was a certain newspaper editor and the endearing way his glasses slipped down his nose. No, that's not all she was thinking about. Paul's kiss burned in her mind, bringing a surge of heat to her cheeks.

"And you're even more beautiful when you blush."

Rodney thought she was blushing because of him. Better not to contradict him, at least not now when he'd taken her hand and was inviting her to join him on the dance floor again.

The floor was packed with other couples, but Rodney led her around them to the center of the room. Was he trying to show her off? Or garner more admiring glances for himself? He'd worn a white jacket that enhanced his considerable tan. And the red tie he sported just happened to match the red of her silk dress.

Rodney drew her near as they danced, one hand splayed on her back. The intimacy of it bothered Susan, as did his off-key humming in her ear. She tried to put a bit of distance between them, but he only held her tighter until she thought she couldn't breathe.

Suddenly she felt as though she had to get out of there, away from the pulsing rhythm of the music and the press of the crowd. Away from Rodney's advances.

"I . . . I'm sorry, Rodney," she stammered. "I need to go home."

His head jerked back and he looked at her sharply. "What? Go home? Why?"

Biting her lip, she averted her eyes from his intense gaze. "I think maybe I drank too much wine. I feel dizzy." That wasn't a lie. She did feel off balance. "I'm sorry, Rodney."

He shrugged, as if to say he would never understand the female sex. "Gee, I thought you were okay. A minute ago you were having a good time and . . ."

He stopped short. Apparently something clicked in his head. "Well, okay, if you feel sick, of course I'll take you home." He gave a nervous chuckle. "I wouldn't want you to faint or anything."

No doubt he feared that she would embarrass him in front of everyone. Most likely he wasn't used to his dates getting ill.

He hurried her off the dance floor, one hand at her waist. Once they were in the lobby, he ordered, "You wait here. I'll go get the car."

After he left, Susan leaned back against the wall, closing her eyes for a moment to still the spinning sensation in her head.

"Susan!" someone squealed loudly beside her ear.

She gasped, her eyes flying open to see who the perpetrator was. "Kristy!" Kristy Jamison, another former classmate at Pitston High. It seemed that running into old acquaintances was becoming a habit.

The tiny blond woman grinned up at Susan. "It's me, only my last name is Beals now. You remember Chad, fullback on the Pirates football team?"

"Sure." She hadn't known either Kristy

or Chad well, though Kristy had been a cheerleader and had gone steady with Chad for as long as Susan could remember. "So you two got married?" Kristy nodded. "And you're living in Gull Harbor now?"

"No. Bayport."

The name of the village sounded familiar to Susan. She believed it was in the northern part of the state, though she wasn't sure.

"We come down here a few times a year to visit some friends," Kristy explained. Her expression changed to one of curiosity. "What's with you and Rodney Silvers?"

The tactless question rankled Susan. "Nothing, Kristy. We're just neighbors."

The brusque reply didn't seem to faze Kristy. She rolled her eyes. "Well, in case you didn't know, Rodney's got about the hottest reputation going around here. Women would die to go out with him," she added, voice lowered dramatically.

Susan almost told Kristy to cut the theatrics. But she suspected there was some truth to the revelation. Innocently she said, "I didn't know that."

Kristy gave a shrill laugh. "Susan, if you're that naïve, then you shouldn't be dating Rodney."

Susan felt as though she'd been baited. She was about to declare that, as a newspaper reporter, she was hardly naïve, when she saw a flash of white outside. It was Rodney's Porsche.

Turning on her heel, she called back to Kristy, "Sorry, Rodney's waiting for me." She noted with satisfaction that Kristy looked peeved.

Susan slid into the passenger seat, welcoming the coolness of the leather upholstery against her skin.

"You're feeling better." Rodney must have noticed the smile on her face.

"Maybe a little," she conceded.

He brightened. "You just needed a little air."

"Possibly." She didn't want him to think she was fully recovered. "But I'm still woozy."

Rodney swung the Porsche out of the parking lot, one hand resting on the stick shift. "I've got just the cure for that."

Susan didn't have the courage to ask what the cure was. Instead, she changed the subject. "You'll never guess who I saw in the lobby."

"Who?" He shifted into a higher gear; the Porsche shuddered in response.

"Kristy Beals."

He glanced at Susan sideways. "Really? I haven't seen Kristy, or Chad, for a while. What's she up to these days?"

The temptation was great to tell Rodney that "what's up" was some hot gossip about him. Resisting the urge, she merely said, "Oh, not much."

Rodney grinned, but didn't reply.

The ride home didn't take long. When he came to her driveway, he didn't stop. "Remember that cure I told you about? Fresh salt air." He winked at her. "And a tour of the *Silver Belle*."

"I don't think so, Rodney, not —"

"Just a quick one," he interrupted. "No more than fifteen minutes." He looked solemn. "I promise."

A small stab of guilt pricked Susan's conscience. Maybe she owed him that much. She certainly hadn't been good company the last couple of hours. Besides, wasn't she curious to see his yacht? "All right. But *just* fifteen minutes."

Revving the Porsche into high gear, Rodney made quick work of the short distance between their cottages.

As soon as they boarded the *Silver Belle*, Susan regretted giving in to him. Not that the sight of the boat rocking gently in the moonlight wasn't impressive. A mild breeze was blowing off the water. The main mast, stripped of its sails, jutted darkly skyward; the wooden deck gleamed in the wash of pallid light.

The scene was so undeniably romantic, it stirred in Susan a longing to be kissed. But that's what she was afraid of — that Rodney would take advantage of the circumstances. He didn't realize she yearned for someone else's lips.

He planted one arm firmly around her waist to guide her below. She went numbly. The cabin was spacious and appointed as she imagined it would be. Oak paneling lined the walls. Besides a wet bar, there was a stereo and a television. "Your yacht is lovely," she managed to say.

"Mmm. I'm so glad you like her." Rodney nuzzled her hair. "Why don't we sit — for just a minute." He beckoned Susan to join him on a small, plush sofa.

She saw his intent clearly — her health was the furthest thing from his mind. "I don't think so, Rodney. I'd really better go home."

His lips curved down in a pout. Yet he persisted. "Come on, Susan. This is part of the cure."

His joke was beginning to wear thin.

"I'm already cured," she shot back. "It was the salt air."

Rodney seemed to perceive her brush-off as teasing. "I'm not talking about *you* this time. I'm the one feeling dizzy. And this is what I need."

His hands gripped her arms and before she could stop him, his mouth came down on hers. Squirming, she tried to break free of his grasp. He held her tighter. Finally, she was able to escape. "No, Rodney!"

He gasped. There was a wild look in his eyes. "What do you mean, Susan?" he demanded.

Kristy hadn't been exaggerating after all. He must be used to getting his way, and this sudden turn of events shocked him. "I'm going home!" Whirling away, Susan raced up the stairs and onto the deck.

Rodney soon came after her. "You can't walk home alone in the dark!"

Susan peered up, her face inches from his. "And why not?" Did he think she was defenseless? "It's a lot safer than having you take me!"

Rodney threw up his arms. "Time out." He worked his tie loose so that it hung crooked. "What did you expect?"

"I expected you to act like a gentleman." Her eyes flashed anger at him.

"I've never had any complaints in that department before."

I'll bet, she wanted to retort. What was the use? He had an enormous ego, fed by hordes of adoring females. "See you around, Rodney."

As she stalked away from him, Rodney called after her, "You can bet on it, Susan. A challenge always excites me."

It seemed she hadn't heard the last from him.

Later, safe in her own bed, Susan tried to sleep and couldn't. She tossed and turned for what seemed like hours. She wanted to forget about her evening with Rodney. She wished she could talk to Paul. That was crazy, she told herself. Her bedside clock read two A.M.

She didn't know his phone number or even where he lived, though she imagined his home to be a tiny apartment somewhere near downtown. She could picture him, eyes heavy with sleep, hair slightly tousled, rousing himself to answer the ringing phone. The image only served to increase her longing. But she could see, too, the startled expression on his face when he heard her voice at the other end.

They'd parted that afternoon on uneasy

terms. He'd found out that she had a date with Rodney and they had fallen into an awkward silence.

If he just knew the truth of how she felt about him. Despite telling herself that she ought to forget about falling in love, it was already too late.

Susan sighed in the darkness. She wondered how much Paul knew of Rodney's reputation. That sort of thing was hard to keep a secret, not that Rodney was apt to try. He probably reveled in his role as play-boy-about-town.

The wind rose outside her cottage, moaning through the trees and grass. Susan shivered, her thoughts suddenly turning to Amy Lambert. It seemed that meeting up with Rodney had been bad news for her in every way. If it wasn't for him, she might never have known that Amy and her mother had lived in this cottage.

Susan turned over. Pressing her face into the pillow, she shut her eyes, determined to make herself go to sleep. She conjured up images of the old newsroom at the *Star*, of Pete, her supervising editor. She let her imagination run free. Pete was giving her an assignment, the most important one she'd ever had, he said soberly. She was to cover the impending visit of the world-famous Nobel Prize–winning poet, Paul Stuart.

Poet? Where had she gotten that? Giggling to herself, Susan reasoned that Paul did publish a poetry column in the *Beacon*. Who knew whether he tried his hand at writing it too? No matter, the ruse seemed to work. She felt herself growing groggy. It wasn't long until she fell asleep, though that sleep was filled with troubling dreams.

Susan didn't remember the dreams when she woke shortly before noon. She just knew she felt weary, as if she hadn't slept at all.

She made herself get up. Padding into the kitchen, she turned on the faucet and set the coffeepot under it. Outside the window, the sky looked overcast again. It would be another gray day.

Determined not to sit around the cottage and mope, she decided it might be a good time to visit the tide pools below Rocky Pointe. She checked a tide chart she'd picked up at Sam's marina. Low tide was at three P.M. *Perfect,* she thought as she measured enough coffee for a pot and made herself scrambled eggs. She'd fix a sandwich for later.

After dressing in a sweatshirt and jeans,

she grabbed a jacket from her closet and put her camera, binoculars, and notebook into her knapsack along with a thermos of coffee and a sandwich. Out on the deck she paused, surveying the ocean. It looked choppy, but not dangerously so. It seemed for a moment that she had forgotten something. But she couldn't think what it might be as she headed up the beach.

"Going out today, Susan?"

Again, Susan was startled by someone coming up behind her. First, it had been Travers, then Kristy, now . . . "Sam!" she said, turning to greet him. "Yes, I am." She chose her words carefully. She had no desire for Paul to get wind of her plans to visit Rocky Pointe. There was a chance Sam would tell Paul if he saw him.

"The sea's kind of rough today." Sam said it casually, but he leveled a long look her way.

"I've seen worse."

"Sure, so have I," he agreed, crossing his arms in front of him. "Where are you headed?"

Susan dropped her knapsack into the bow of the *Anne Marie*. "Just up the coast a little way. I wanted to check out a couple of places for tide pools."

Sam didn't reply.

"I'd better head out, I guess, if I want to get back before dark."

"I reckon you had. Remember now what I told you the other day."

She knew he was talking about the men who had harassed her. It was funny; she hadn't even thought of them. "I will, Sam. If they so much as give me one high sign, I'll let you know."

He seemed satisfied with that. Helping her into the boat, he waited until she was seated, then untied the vessel from its moorings. "Take care," he cautioned.

Susan waved to Sam as she steered the *Anne Marie* into open water.

The farther Susan went toward Rocky Pointe, the rougher the sea was. The air was chillier too, causing her to don her jacket. But the trip was worth it. She knew that as soon as the lighthouse came into view.

It was swaddled in mist, windows darkened, like a great, silent sentinel in a bleak land. Fog rose and curled over it and the rocks below. Yet Susan could see well enough that she wasn't afraid of losing her sense of direction on the way home. But the fog would bear watching. If it thickened, she'd head back to the marina.

Susan stared at the lighthouse for several minutes. Detecting no sign of life there, she set about the task she'd come to Rocky Pointe for.

The tide pools proved to be just as fascinating as they'd been the first time she had seen them. And though the lighthouse was equally intriguing to her, it wasn't long before she became so busy writing notes and taking pictures that she forgot Daryl Travers could be watching her from one of those blank windows.

Time passed too quickly. Susan hated to take a break, but she was forced to. Her fingers were cramped from so much writing and she needed to stretch her legs.

She decided to climb up the rocks for a better view of the ocean — and of the lighthouse, if she was truthful. She found a flat spot and sat down, placing her knapsack beside her. She took out her sandwich and ate it, then had a cup of coffee. The hot liquid felt good going down, warming her.

Idly she picked up her binoculars. Lifting them to her eyes, she trained them on the lighthouse. Fog still enveloped the rocks, but the tower rose above it in clear view. Susan remembered the harrowing tales Paul had told her of shipwrecks and heroic rescues. She wondered when the light had been built and how many men had been saved by its beacon guiding their ships through the treacherous straits.

She felt sad that the light would never see duty again. Turning her head, she let her gaze rove over the keeper's quarters. It was a low building with windows in a row along one side. The keeper and his family, if he had been married, would have had an extraordinary view of the ocean.

There were still curtains at two of the windows. They'd been pulled shut, probable evidence of Travers's love of privacy. Susan started to lower the binoculars when something at one of the windows caught her attention, sending a shiver up her spine. Had one of those curtains *moved?*

She riveted her attention on it. Was Travers there after all? Or had the wind entered through a crack in the window to ruffle the thin-looking material?

There was movement again. This time, Susan was certain of it, and what happened next made her blood turn ice-cold in her veins, even as her heart pumped furiously. Her breath came in constricted gasps as a face wavered into view. Not

Travers's, but a child's, beautiful as heaven must be.

"Amy." The whispered utterance was her own, but Susan didn't hear it. The face fled from sight as easily as it had appeared, elusive as the mist.

Susan couldn't move. She felt frozen to the ground, one frantic thought in her mind, one prayer on her lips: to see that little face again.

She kept her binoculars trained on the darkened square of glass for what seemed hours. But there was nothing except her own sense of despair.

Then an image of Daryl Travers invaded her head, as horrifying as the child's was innocent. Had he kidnapped Amy? Was he holding her prisoner in his lighthouse? It was unthinkable, yet it might not be un-reasonable.

Susan had no answers; she only knew what she had seen. *Had* the face been Amy's? How many times had she believed she'd spotted Joey during those difficult months? Her mind ticked them off. In Cherrystone Mall; on a crowded bus; at Willowby Park. The list could go on and on. Was the same thing happening now? But she had seen *someone* each of those times, a child, though none of them had been Joey. Was what she'd witnessed today only a deception, a trick of her mind?

Stop it! Susan scolded herself as she deliberately turned away from the lighthouse and started her descent down the steep rocks to where she'd left the *Anne Marie*. Then she stopped. If Amy was inside the keeper's house, if there was any chance, any chance at all, to capture the child's face on film. . . .

Susan knew she had to take that chance. Scrambling back up the rocks, she rummaged in the knapsack for her camera. Stealthily she approached the area just outside Travers's high fence. Grass grew there, as did clusters of small trees, stunted by the wind.

She positioned herself near a stand of tall bushes, angling for the best view of the window where she'd seen the face. An eternity passed and nothing moved. The curtain was motionless.

But the fog she'd been watching all afternoon was growing more dense by the minute. Susan knew she had to leave, or risk not finding her way to the marina.

She was about to pack up her camera when she sensed she wasn't alone. There was a dead calm, but the atmosphere around her was threatening, as if the fog had finally taken on a sinister shape of its own making, with huge hands that sought to reach out and steal her very life.

Just as she took a careful step, the calm was shattered by the voice she had begged not to hear.

"Planning on taking a few pictures, little lady?"

Chapter Seven

"Mr. Travers." Susan was shocked at the calmness of her voice, as though she were greeting a pleasant acquaintance instead of the man she now viewed as her enemy. But when she turned to face him and found herself staring down the long end of a rifle, she gasped.

Travers's mouth curved up in a surly smile. "It seems we meet again, newspaper lady." He advanced on her rapidly, his smile gone. "You didn't answer my question!"

Susan jerked back in reaction to the harsh demand. "I was just . . . admiring your lighthouse, Mr. Travers." She hated patronizing him that way, but what choice did she have? She wasn't sure her knees would bear up if she tried to run. And how could she do battle with a madman and his cocked weapon?

"I'll bet you were." He spat on the ground in front of her. "Don't play coy with me. Can't you read? Keep out!"

The roar of his voice echoed off the rocks, fading in the fast-encroaching fog. "Of course I can read." Susan raised herself to full height, but inside she was trembling. If the face she had seen in the window was real, then far more than her own safety was at stake. "There's no need to shout, Mr. Travers. No need for that, either." She pointed at the gun.

Travers gave a short laugh. "Is that so, Miss Miles? Or should I call you Susan?" he asked in a rough whisper. Eyes locked with hers, he took a menacing step toward her.

The breath checked in Susan's throat. She forced it out. "I want you to know that I had no intention of trespassing on your property."

Travers's eyebrows shot up, but he lowered the rifle a fraction. It was now pointed at her stomach instead of her heart. "Just trying to live dangerously then." His one hand reached out to stroke the barrel of the weapon.

Susan shivered at the gesture. She almost bolted, but something made her stay. "I'm not the type who enjoys living dangerously. Are you, Mr. Travers?" She said it as if she believed he would agree with her.

He wavered. It was just for an instant, but she saw his uncertainty. She felt she'd won a tiny victory, though her nerves were as tense as drawn wire.

Travers swaggered nearer, no doubt trying to gain any ground he thought he might have lost. "I would advise you to be on your way now, Miss Miles. And I wouldn't plan on coming back."

Susan demurred. "All right." Gathering her courage, she turned from him and began the long descent down the rocks. Any instant she expected to hear the sharp report of the rifle and feel the searing pain in her flesh that would tell her he'd only been waiting for his chance.

She slowly measured her steps. If she did start to run, might it trigger some response in him that would cause him to shoot at her or come after her?

The journey seemed to take an eternity. Finally Susan reached the spot where she'd left the *Anne Marie*. Travers hadn't fired the gun, nor had he followed her, as she discovered when she dared to glance behind her. The only sound she detected was the slight creaking of the *Anne Marie* as it rocked on the waves.

Scrambling into the boat, she started the engine. The wind had died down, so the sails would be useless. Besides, the engine would make for a quicker getaway. Resisting the temptation to look back again, Susan guided the boat out to sea, almost crying with relief.

"You look like you could use a cup of tea, dear."

Anna Winston's kindly voice penetrated Susan's dreamlike state. With no more than an hour's fitful sleep the night before, it was little wonder. "Yes, I believe I could, Anna." Susan forced a smile.

Anna peered at her, brows furrowed. "Are you feeling well, Susan? You look a bit pale."

"I'm fine."

The older woman merely frowned as she left Susan for a moment to get the tea. Susan sagged back in her chair, fingers pressed to her forehead. Covering one of Gull Harbor's high social events was the last thing she wanted to do that afternoon, though she had been looking forward to the prospect a couple of days ago. That was before she'd become consumed with morbid thoughts of Daryl Travers and his rifle, of a darkened lighthouse window and a little girl's face.

"Here you are." Susan felt a cup and

saucer being pressed into her hands.

Anna seated herself on the chair beside Susan's. "You need a bite to eat too." She held out a plate with several dainty cakes on it.

Susan took a petit four, though she doubted she could get it down. Her appetite had fled. "Thank you, Anna."

"Perhaps Paul is expecting too much of you, dear." Anna raised her teacup to her lips, sipping slowly. "Even though he is a nice young man." She smiled sweetly at Susan over the rim of her cup.

"No, Paul's not making me work too hard." That was true. Besides, work was hardly the thing uppermost in her mind these days.

Anna leaned close. "If you ask me, Paul's taken on quite a load, running the *Beacon* all by himself. Well, not quite all by himself, now that he's got you, dear." Anna beamed and took a bite of chocolate-frosted cake. "Doesn't Ruth give a lovely party?"

"Yes, lovely," Susan had to agree, glancing around. She'd been dutifully taking notes since she set foot in Ruth Westman's spacious Cape Cod–style home. And she'd been impressed with the ambience and warmth of both the house and its owner.

The parlor where she and Anna were seated was tastefully furnished with vintage sofas and chairs. Tall vases of daisies and chrysanthemums lent splashes of bright color to the room.

Most of the ladies in attendance appeared to be in their fifties and sixties. They had come dressed for the occasion in silk afternoon dresses and designer suits. All of them had been accommodating as she'd circulated among them, taking pictures. Normally she would have enjoyed covering such an event. *Normally.*

"It's the highlight of the year," Anna declared. "Everyone who is anyone is at Ruth's tea." Her face wore a proud expression. Then she grew sober again as she studied Susan. "I don't mean to harp on this, dear, but you do look like you need a good rest."

Susan sighed, putting down her cup and saucer. "Yes, I suppose I do," she admitted at last. Raising her eyes to meet Anna's, she searched the older woman's face for courage to somehow broach the subject that was on her mind. Finally she said, "Anna, this is probably a strange thing to ask, but did you know a young woman named Chris Lambert and her daughter, Amy?"

Anna's eyes grew wide. Her hands trembled slightly as they gripped the cup. "Why do you ask?"

Susan leaned forward. "A neighbor of mine told me about them. You see, I live in the cottage where Chris and Amy used to live."

"Oh, my!" Anna gasped, looking away.

Susan suspected from Anna's reaction that the older woman must have known Chris and Amy Lambert. Of course, the kidnapping would have been the talk of the village for the past months. Though she didn't want to distress Anna, Susan pressed on. "I'm sorry, but it's just that I've been troubled ever since I learned about Amy's disappearance, and I . . ."

Anna looked so stricken that Susan couldn't continue. She reached out to pat the older woman's arm. "I didn't mean to upset you."

Anna shook her head. "No. It's all right." Gazing out a nearby window, she said, "It was such a tragedy, Susan. Everyone in Gull Harbor was . . ." She smiled, lower lip quivering. "Everyone was simply aghast over the news."

Not half as aghast as they'd be if they had seen what I did, Susan thought, wishing she could spill out her experience to Anna. But

Anna's mood suddenly seemed to shift. Instead of horror, her face wore a look of wonderment.

Susan chided herself for bringing up such a difficult subject with a woman who apparently believed that teddy bears were human. Who knew what conclusions Anna had come to on the case? "I'm sure people were stunned," she said in delayed response. Anna nodded silently. Susan realized she couldn't risk further upsetting Anna by mentioning Travers's name or even Rocky Pointe, let alone what she'd seen in the lighthouse window. Still, the mystery remained about why Anna had been so fearful of Travers. Was it due to no more than a mix-up on an order, as she and Paul had discussed?

Susan felt Anna's hand on her arm. "Oh, do let's talk of other things, dear."

"Yes."

"Have you seen Ruth's bears?"

"No, I haven't." Anna had already risen from her chair. Susan followed.

Anna's eyes lit up with childlike eagerness. "Then you must come with me. I'm positive Damien, Cecilia, and Howard will be thrilled to make your acquaintance."

The words on the computer screen in

front of Susan seemed to blur together. She rubbed her eyes. Her lack of sleep was quickly catching up on her. Her watch told her it was quarter past seven.

At least she had managed to make a graceful exit from the tea after Ruth had invited Anna to help gather up the cups and saucers from the serving table. And she had completed and entered her report on the social. But she still had to finish her story on the environmentalists' rally, and it was going badly. Words wouldn't jell into sentences.

Besides, Paul hadn't showed up and all sorts of things had gone through her head as to why. Maybe he hated facing her as her employer, realizing it would be awkward for them after the intimate kiss they had shared.

He might also have mistaken ideas about how her date with Rodney had gone, particularly if he was aware of Rodney's playboy reputation.

Or possibly his feelings for her weren't as intense as he'd led her to believe. Had he only been moved by her sympathetic reaction to his loss of someone he'd truly loved?

Susan put her head in her hands. She was driving herself crazy with speculation.

Yet she was desperate to see Paul. Today she was the one who could use some sympathy.

She needed to tell him about her visit to Rocky Pointe, even if he gave her a lecture for breaking her promise to him. She needed, too, for him to take her in his arms so that she might feel the comforting warmth of his palms on her back as he whispered that everything would be all right.

She closed her eyes. If she rested for just a few minutes, her vision might clear and her mind might stop its racing from one thought to another. She took a slow, deep breath. The tension in her body began to ease.

The next thing Susan was aware of was a hand on her shoulder. She raised her head with a start. "Mr. Tra . . ." she stammered. Forcing her eyes open, she brushed strands of hair away from her line of vision. "Paul?"

Had she been asleep? Was the man standing beside her really Paul? She had been dreaming of Daryl Travers, she was certain now. Had *she* been his captive, not Amy? She couldn't remember the details of the dream, only that she had been frightened.

"Susan?"

The softly spoken word drew her attention again. As her eyes focused, she saw Paul gazing at her worriedly.

"Are you okay?" He bent over her, but he withdrew his hand from her shoulder, resting it on her desk. "You look beat."

Susan suddenly felt ashamed that he had caught her sleeping. Maybe he thought she and Rodney had been out partying the night before. "I'm fine. Just a bit tired."

He frowned at her. "More than a bit, I'd say."

"I'm sorry I dozed off."

He glanced away briefly, but his eyes came back to her. "What's wrong, Susan?"

Her heart gave a loud slam in her chest, and she wondered if he could hear it. Now that he was here, looking at her this way, the words that had burned in her mind all day fled. But he didn't give up; he continued to pin her with that electric gaze.

"There is something," she said at last, dropping her eyes.

"Do you want to tell me?"

From the resignation in his voice, she was certain he'd come to the wrong conclusion. He thought she cared for Rodney and didn't know how to tell him. She should make it clear to Paul that she was falling in love with him, not Rodney. She couldn't. Maybe it was the more formal setting of the office that made her say, "I do need to talk, but I haven't finished my assignments. You said I have to have them in by nine, and it's nearly eight now."

Paul's mouth curved up slightly. "The nine o'clock deadline isn't written in stone."

Susan gave him a tentative smile. "I'd still like to meet it. Would you have time afterward? I mean, to talk?"

"Of course I have time," he said quietly, regarding her for another moment. Then he straightened, his demeanor all business. "Well, I've got a story to finish too, so I'll let you get back to yours."

For the next hour, it was as if each was determined to ignore the other's presence as they furiously typed and printed out their reports. But Susan knew it was only a facade. She could no more forget Paul was in the office than she could forget to breathe. Her thoughts automatically went to him and she found herself sending covetous looks his way, though he didn't appear to notice.

But when they both finally finished their tasks, Susan saw her own profound relief reflected in his eyes as she handed him her stories.

Paul laid them on his desk along with the roll of film she'd given him from the social. "Now we'll talk. I don't have to be back until midnight."

He turned abruptly, heading for the door. Susan hurried to catch up. "Midnight? Why do you have to come back then?"

"We print," he said simply.

"Oh." Her cheeks flushed with embarrassment, but a blast of chill wind fanned them as she stepped outside the office. "Is there anyplace open? I mean, somewhere we could have privacy."

"The Gull Café. It's not far."

"Sounds good." She didn't tell him that the unpleasant receptionist at the Higgins Agency had recommended the café.

The restaurant was small — no more than eight booths and a few tables. As they walked in, Susan saw that she and Paul had the place to themselves. He led her to one of the back booths.

After they were seated, a waitress appeared with menus. Susan opened hers. Though she still wasn't hungry, she thought she should eat something. "What's good?" She peered at Paul over the menu.

"The chili. Best I've ever had."

"Okay. I'll have that." Despite the way

she felt, Susan couldn't help smiling. With his head bent, Paul's glasses had slipped again.

Instead of adjusting them, he took them off and laid them on the table. She remembered what had happened after he'd done that a couple of days ago.

The waitress came and took their orders, quickly returning with two huge, steaming bowls.

"I gather they must make chili by the gallon here." Susan picked a packet of crackers from a dish on the table and tore it open.

Paul concentrated on stirring his spoon through the thick mixture of meat and beans. "We didn't come here to discuss the cuisine," he said at last.

"No." She sighed, carefully crushing the crackers over the top of her chili. "Paul, yesterday I went back to Rocky Pointe."

Her direct approach had the expected effect. Paul stared at her, a spoonful of chili poised halfway to his mouth. He dropped the spoon back into the bowl. "Why did you do that, Susan?" His eyes narrowed.

Her defenses rose automatically, and she had to stifle the impulse to tell him it was her business why she did what she did. But his distress was so plainly obvious, his feelings for her so naked in his eyes, that she couldn't be angry. Besides, now she knew that he had genuine reason to be concerned.

"Susan?" He appealed to her, reaching for her hand.

She put her spoon aside. "I thought I was going to study the tide pools. But I'm afraid the real reason I went had more to do with Travers's lighthouse."

Paul's fingers gripped hers. "You went up to the lighthouse?"

Susan shook her head. "No, not exactly. I was taking a break from my research, having a sandwich not too far from the light. I'd brought my binoculars and happened to focus them on the tower, then . . . the keeper's house." She looked away.

"Go on."

She searched Paul's face for a moment. "In one of the windows of the keeper's house, I thought that . . ." She hesitated, then started over. "There were curtains at the window. One of them seemed to move slightly. I wasn't sure, so I kept watching, wondering why the curtain had moved if the place was abandoned."

"Susan, are you trying to tell me that you saw something at the lighthouse window?"

"Yes," she whispered.

"Some people say that Rocky Pointe is haunted. But you don't believe in such things as ghosts, do you?"

She shook her head. "When the curtain drew back again, I saw a face. Amy Lambert's face."

"No!" Paul paled visibly.

"Yes, I'm positive," she said vehemently, withdrawing her hand from his. It was obvious he didn't believe her, and it hurt.

Paul's eyes took on a distant look. "Amy couldn't be in Travers's lighthouse."

"Why not?" Susan suddenly realized their argument had drawn the unwanted attention of the waitress. Her voice lowered but no less urgent, she asked, "Why couldn't Travers have kidnapped the child, Paul?" Glancing back at the waitress, she saw the woman had turned away.

"It's impossible because . . ." He didn't finish, only took her hand again. Slowly he interlaced her fingers with his. "Did you see Travers too?" he whispered.

Susan latched onto Paul's small concession. Maybe he didn't think she was crazy, after all. Still, she hesitated.

"You saw him." Paul's jaw was set. "Did Travers hurt you? Threaten you?" he asked grimly.

She avoided Paul's eyes. "He didn't hurt me, just told me not to come back."

"Susan, you've got to talk to Sheriff Glendig."

She knew he was right, but she already dreaded it. She had her own notions of what the sheriff was like. Looking up, she pleaded, "Not tonight."

Paul gave her a sympathetic smile. "How about tomorrow morning at the *Beacon* office? I'll arrange it."

"All right. Will you be there?" she asked hopefully.

"Of course." He squeezed her hand, then released it. "We'd better eat our chili."

"You mean it's not best when it's cold?" Her lame attempt at humor fell flat and they both grew silent as they concentrated on their food. Finally Susan put down her spoon. "Did you know Chris Lambert?"

Paul wiped his mouth carefully on his napkin. "Not personally. I interviewed her after the kidnapping."

"I'll bet she was almost hysterical after losing Amy."

"Strange you should say that." Paul fiddled with his spoon, then put it back into his now-empty bowl. "I'm sure Chris loved her daughter, or at least it's safe to assume she did. But during the couple of interviews I did with her, she seemed, well, distracted, for lack of a better word."

"She was likely in shock, don't you think?"

He shrugged. "Probably." He picked up his glasses and cleaned them with a tissue. "Or maybe she felt guilty, hating herself for letting Amy out of her sight."

Susan thought of Stephanie Peterson's anguished face, her tear-swollen eyes. "Any mother who loves her child wouldn't give up, Paul."

"I'm sure Chris hasn't given up."

"Where is she now?"

Paul looked thoughtful. "Somewhere out of state, living with relatives, I understand."

"You haven't talked to her lately?"

"No."

"But Sheriff Glendig and Detective Osborn must know where she is."

Paul picked up his glasses again. "I couldn't tell you that. I wish I knew."

Distracted for a moment as she watched him slide the glasses over the bridge of his nose, Susan said finally, "I know someone who's very upset over Amy's disappearance."

"Who?"

"Anna Winston."

Paul smiled. "I'm not surprised. But how did you find out?"

"I was talking to her at the tea this afternoon and I brought up the subject of Chris and Amy." She touched his arm. "Paul, she looked stricken."

"Anna baby-sat for Chris a lot these past few years, so it isn't any wonder." He folded his napkin and put his spoon on it. "You might have noticed that Anna gets a little . . . mixed up at times. She no doubt thought of Amy as a granddaughter. Anna told me once that she'd never had children."

"She talks to her bears as if they're her children," Susan offered.

"That's true."

They both laughed, but the mood that had been struck was melancholy. Susan wished it didn't have to be that way, not when her heart only wanted to dwell on the more captivating aspects of her relationship with Paul — like the little quiver that overtook her whenever he touched her.

She suspected he felt the same way, though there was a flicker of uncertainty in his eyes. That reminded her that he hadn't forgotten about Rodney.

She made a bold decision. Clearing her throat, she said, "In case you'd like to know, Paul, I'm not —"

"Sorry, closing time."

Susan let out a little gasp. The waitress had seemingly appeared out of nowhere with her pointed announcement.

Paul looked at his watch. "It's eleven o'clock." Getting up from the booth, he took the check from the waitress and handed her several bills. "My treat," he said to Susan.

"Thanks, Paul." She regretted the waitress's interruption, not sure if she could work up the courage to finish telling Paul what she'd started to say.

Outside the café, they headed back in the direction of the *Beacon* office. The street was deserted. "Where's your car parked?" Paul asked.

"Half a block from the office." She had a sudden idea. "Would you like me to stay and help you get ready for printing?" As soon as the words were out, she regretted how eager she sounded.

"You need your sleep."

Didn't he want her to stay? "Of course, you're right, Paul." She was bone-tired, but she dreaded going back to her cottage and being alone with only her thoughts for company.

They reached her car. Paul waited while she unlocked the door. Just as she was sliding behind the wheel, he announced, "Susan, I've got bad news."

Her heart sank. "What is it?"

"You've got a flat tire."

"What!" Jumping out of the car, she looked where he was pointing. The left front tire drooped against the pavement. "How could that have happened?"

"I don't know." Paul hunkered down beside the wheel. He ran his hand along the exposed tread. "You might have picked up a nail or piece of glass. Do you have a spare?"

"That is the spare, Paul."

"Oh," was all he said.

"Don't worry. You have to get back to the office. I'll go to the café and call a service station."

She heard him chuckle. "The café's closed, remember? And it wouldn't do any good to call, anyway. The one service station in Gull Harbor closes at eight on Sundays."

"Then I'll get a taxi." She peered nervously at Paul. He was grinning.

"According to my sources, there hasn't been a taxi service in Gull Harbor since nineteen forty-five."

Susan threw up her hands. "Well, then, I'll . . ." It looked as if she had run out of options. Paul's face still wore a grin. "I hate to ask you this, but do you think you might be able to drive me home? I know you have a deadline to meet and —"

"I'm more than able to drive you home." He took hold of her hand, leading her in the opposite direction. "The tire can be fixed tomorrow. And in case you weren't aware, you're much more important to me than a deadline."

She couldn't think of a reply, though the comment caused her heart to miss a beat.

Chapter Eight

The house was dark as Paul pulled into the driveway. Above, the sky wore a thick layer of clouds, hiding the moon and stars, and the cottage was only a hazy image against the black outline of the trees. Susan realized with chagrin that she had forgotten to leave a light on, as she usually did when she knew she'd be coming home late.

Paul cut the engine and she turned to thank him for the ride. But he was already getting out of his side of the car. "I'll walk you up," he said before she could protest.

Secretly Susan was glad for his company. The air smelled heavy with moisture, almost oppressive, and she was more conscious of how secluded her cottage was.

The only sound she could hear was the faint roar of the ocean. Opening her purse, she fished for her keys.

"Need a light?" Paul asked. He'd come to stand beside her. Soon a thin, bright beam shone on her purse; he was holding a penlight.

"Thanks." She smiled, wishing she could see his face better. Her keys glinted in the light as she took them out.

"You're welcome," he replied. "Susan . . ."

"What, Paul?" She sensed he took a step closer.

"At the café, you started to tell me something when the waitress interrupted. You never finished." He paused again to lay the penlight on the hood of his car. "I don't think it was about Travers or Amy."

"You're right. It wasn't." She regarded him. His face was visible now, though his eyes were veiled in shadow. "It was about us, or . . ." She faltered when his hands came to rest on her shoulders.

"Rodney?" There was a hint of trepidation in his voice even as his face drew close to hers.

She wound her arms around his neck, pleased that he trembled a little in response. "Paul, my date with Rodney was, well, a flop."

"It was?"

He sounded disbelieving, which made her smile. "Uh-huh. Poor Rodney couldn't understand why I wasn't impressed with him. But it was all your fault."

"My fault?"

"Of course. I was distracted, thinking

about you the whole evening. Rodney didn't stand a chance."

His mouth brushed her forehead. "I can't say I feel sorry for Rodney." His fingers combed through her hair. "On second thought, I feel very sorry for him. He doesn't know what he's missing."

Paul whispered her name and she turned slightly so that their lips met in a long, searching kiss. Finally she pulled back. "I'd better go in. And you've got to get the *Beacon* printed."

"You keep reminding me," he said huskily, as if he didn't care just then to concentrate on such practical matters. But he broke away to retrieve his penlight. Shining it on the path ahead of them, he took her hand and they walked together to the front door.

As soon as he trained the light on the door, Susan saw that something was wrong. She drew in a sharp breath. "Paul!" She clutched his arm. "It's already open."

He traced around the frame with the light. "Are you sure you locked it?"

"Yes." She lowered her voice to a whisper as fear gripped her. "Someone's broken in."

"Maybe," he said, voice lowered. "Wait

here." He killed the light.

"Where are you going?"

"To check things out."

"What if whoever broke in is still inside?" Her hold on him tightened.

"I'll be all right."

He sounded confident, but she wasn't taking any chances. "I'm going with you."

"I want you to stay here, Susan."

"And I said I'm going with you," she answered stubbornly.

He sighed. "Okay. But stay behind me."

Slowly Paul pushed the door open; it groaned.

"Well, they know we're here." Her off-hand remark drew a short laugh from him.

"Take hold of my coat," he ordered close to her ear.

Obediently she took hold, letting him lead her along. If she'd thought it was dark outside, she was unprepared for the pitch blackness of the interior of the cottage.

"Ouch!"

Susan jumped at the loud cry. "What?" She tugged at Paul's coat, alarmed. There was no answer. "Paul?" Her voice rose in panic.

"I stubbed my foot on something," came the muffled reply.

"Oh." She was sorry about the injury,

but relieved that it wasn't worse.

"Susan?"

"Yes?"

"I don't think there's anyone here but us." The penlight came on again. "Where's a lamp?"

"Here." She groped for a moment and found the wall switch that turned on the ceiling light.

After her eyes adjusted to the brightness, she exclaimed, "Oh, Paul!" Her hands flew to her face. The place was a complete mess. The sofa pillows were strewn on the floor. A chair was overturned; one of the lamps was shattered.

She hardly knew that Paul's arms came around her to hold her. He murmured words she didn't hear. "Why? Why would anyone do this?" she asked, grasping at him for support.

He rocked her for a moment. "I don't know." He leaned back so that she saw his face. "Over the past year, there've been break-ins at several of the cottages in this area. Burglars, looking for anything of value."

"I don't have anything of value," she said, then realized immediately that she did. "My camera!"

"Where'd you leave it?" His gaze swept

the room, as if he might locate the object in the chaos.

Then she remembered. "Paul, the camera's in my car." She looked away. "I'm sorry."

"Don't be sorry." His arm stayed firmly at her waist. "Anyone would be upset. Come on," he urged. "Let's check the other rooms."

Susan's worst fears were confirmed. The whole place had been ransacked, though the kitchen had been partially spared. Just the lower drawers and cabinets lay tipped over, their contents strewn on the floor.

In the bedroom, the mattress was off the bed, the chest of drawers toppled.

"We have to call Sheriff Glendig, Susan. Where's your phone?"

"In the living room," she said mechanically, sitting down on what was left of the bed.

"The phone's okay, at least," she heard Paul say from the living room. His conversation with the sheriff was indistinct; she wasn't up to straining to hear what he told the law officer.

After he finished, he came back into the bedroom and sat down beside her. "The sheriff and his detective will be out shortly. I woke him up." Paul smiled briefly as he brought his hand up to her cheek. "And you won't have to worry about me going back to the office."

"Why not?"

"I talked to Steven too. The beast is down again."

"No!" Looking up at Paul, she saw that he didn't appear in the least upset.

He invited her to lean her head against his shoulder. "So, we print tomorrow night and the paper's a day late," he said matter-of-factly.

"Is it the new part that's broken?" She felt him give a little shrug.

"Steven doesn't know yet. But it's not likely."

"Why?"

"Because it's under warranty. The rest of the beast isn't."

Susan giggled despite her own dire circumstances. "I'm so glad you're here," she whispered, pressing her lips to his ear.

His fingers caressed her arm. "If you hadn't been with me tonight, if we hadn't stopped at the café, you might . . ." His voice trailed off.

She hushed him. "Don't say it, Paul." Nestling her head back against his shoulder, she reminded him, "I'm safe. We're safe. That's all that matters."

It *was* all that mattered. If anything had been stolen from her cottage, she wouldn't miss it. And the way Paul was holding her, she felt as though she could read his thoughts. Things could be replaced; people couldn't.

The pulsing flash of blue and white lights outside signaled the arrival of Sheriff Glendig. "They're here," Paul announced. He helped her off the bed and together they met the sheriff and his detective at the front door.

Susan was surprised to see that Glen Glendig was tall and thin, with an angular face. He looked nothing like she'd pictured. His eyes met hers with an almost soulful expression, and he didn't smile when Paul introduced her.

The detective was just the opposite in appearance: short and plump, with a ruddy complexion. He gave Susan a wide smile.

Sheriff Glendig took out a pad and pencil. "What happened here?" he asked.

Susan felt Paul's hand at her shoulder. "When I got home a few minutes ago, I . . . we found the lock on the front door broken. Obviously someone broke in."

The sheriff shot her a look that she couldn't quite interpret. He turned to Detective Osborn. "Check it," he ordered.

Susan watched as the detective took something from a small case he was carrying. Then he started dusting around the door for fingerprints.

"Now then, when did you leave home and what time did you return?"

Her attention was drawn back to the sheriff. "I left at one-thirty." She paused, frowning.

"We got here at approximately quarter to twelve," Paul put in.

The sheriff jotted some notes. "Did you touch anything after you came in?" He again directed the question to Susan.

"No, other than the light switch on the wall." She remembered something else. "We did sit on the bed for a few minutes before you came."

A half-smile twitched at one corner of the sheriff's mouth. Susan wondered what he was thinking.

"Any of your possessions missing that you can see?" he asked.

"I haven't checked around yet. The place is pretty much a mess."

"That's obvious," the sheriff said sardonically. "What about your television? Stereo?"

"I don't own either one."

The detective stopped his dusting and

turned toward her. Both he and the sheriff gave her an odd look. It made her feel as though they thought she were the criminal instead of the victim.

"We've had a few burglaries out this way in the past months," Sheriff Glendig said at last. "Haven't caught anyone yet, but we suspect it's teenagers. Looking for drug money, likely."

The supposition didn't put Susan's mind at ease. What if she had been home when the thief or thieves happened by? Would they have harmed her? She thought of Marion's question about her living alone. No doubt the woman was aware of the burglaries. Maybe she'd almost let the information slip, then caught herself, not wanting to lose a tenant.

Then Susan thought of Daryl Travers. Wasn't he a far more serious threat to her than some kid who wanted to steal a television? She knew she had to tell Sheriff Glendig about her experience at Rocky Pointe, but something in her rebelled against it. Looking at Paul, she wondered if he would bring up the subject now, while the law officer was here.

He didn't. Nor did he say much at all as the sheriff and his detective conducted a walk-through of the cottage. He loaned her his silent support instead, holding her hand, giving her encouraging glances.

"Did you know your back door's open?"

Sheriff Glendig's question startled Susan. She watched as he swung the door back on its hinges. "You mean the lock's broken on it too?"

After a quick inspection, the sheriff pronounced, "No, it's fine. You must not have locked it when you left today."

Susan couldn't believe her carelessness. Had she really forgotten?

"If it was never locked, then why would someone go to the trouble of breaking in the front?" That came from Paul.

She looked at him, then turned back to the sheriff. "Yes, why didn't they just walk in through this door?"

The law officer shrugged. "I can't answer that."

By this time, Detective Osborn had come into the kitchen. He set about dusting around the open door. "We'll do our best to find out," he offered, directing a quick smile at Susan.

She decided she liked the detective, but she couldn't say the same for his boss. Of course, that was hardly a surprise to her. "Will I be allowed to clean up some of this mess tonight?"

"Just as soon as Detective Osborn checks for prints in the bedroom." The sheriff snapped shut his notebook and left the kitchen.

Paul turned her toward him. "I'm staying with you, Susan, to help you clean up."

She started to protest, but a commotion coming from the direction of the living room drew her attention.

The next instant, Rodney burst into the kitchen. He had a frenzied look on his face.

"Rodney! What are you doing here?" She didn't know who was more surprised — herself, Paul, or Rodney.

Rodney marched over to her. His hair was blown, and though he had on a dress shirt and blazer, the first two buttons on the shirt were undone. His tie was askew. From his reputation, Susan thought she knew why.

"What happened?" he demanded. "My gosh, your place looks like a tornado struck."

"Close." She studied his disheveled appearance, tempted to say that he must have been caught in the same tornado. But the lipstick stain on his collar confirmed her first suspicion. "Why are you here, Rodney?"

"I saw the lights on the cruiser outside. I was scared to death that something had happened to you." He blinked as if he had just noticed Paul. "Stuart," he said flatly in acknowledgement.

"Silvers." Paul's reply was equally curt.

Susan felt Paul's arm come around her waist. "I'm fine, Rodney. Someone broke in while I was away."

Rodney reached out to take her hand. "You can't stay here alone." Ignoring Paul, he said, "Let me be with you, Susan. You'll be safe with me."

She almost laughed at his dramatic appeal. But was he oblivious to the sudden electricity in the air? Didn't he see the way Paul had drawn her possessively closer? She was about to tell him that she was well taken care of, thank you, when Paul spoke up.

"There's no need for you to stay, Silvers. I'll be with Susan for as long as she needs someone."

Rodney reacted swiftly. He pinned Susan with his dark eyes, as if to say. *You wouldn't choose him over me, would you?*

She smiled sweetly. "See, Rodney? There's no need for you to worry. Thanks anyway for your offer."

His mouth opened, but nothing came

out. After an awkward moment, he backed away. "Okay. See you around then, Susan."

She couldn't help giggling a little at his hasty exit. But when Paul tilted her face so their eyes met, she saw he was serious. "I meant that, Susan. I'm not leaving you tonight."

The sheriff and his detective came back before she could reply. They informed her they would be on their way. The sheriff told her that he wanted to see her again after she'd had a chance to clean up the cottage.

The law officer was turning to go when Susan stopped him. "Sheriff Glendig, I . . ." Paul squeezed her hand. "There's another matter, an urgent matter, I'd like to talk to you about."

The sheriff leveled a cool gaze her way. "What is it?"

Paul stepped forward. "I think what Susan means is that if it's convenient for you, could you stop by my office sometime this afternoon?"

Though she was used to speaking for herself, Susan sent Paul a grateful glance. At that early hour of the morning, she was not in the mood to tell the sheriff her theories about the disappearance of Amy Lambert.

Sheriff Glendig nodded. "I'll be there at two." He motioned to his detective and they left.

Susan stood, leaning against Paul, eyes closed, for several moments. "You're exhausted," he admonished.

Even those few hushed words seemed unnaturally loud in the quiet that had descended now that the law officers and Rodney were gone. "But, Paul, I've got to clean up the cottage." She gestured weakly toward the upset drawers. Her arm felt weightless.

The truth was, she was more than tired. Her bones must have turned to jelly. But she wasn't prepared for the terrible wave of dizziness and nausea that gripped her.

She grabbed Paul. His arms caught her. "I think I'm going to be sick."

"Lean on me," he ordered softly. "I'll help you to the bathroom."

She got there just in time. As soon as Paul closed the door behind her, she lost her dinner. Perspiration broke out on her forehead; her hands shook. She waited until the feeling of sickness passed. Then she splashed cold water on her face and rinsed her mouth.

Glimpsing herself in the mirror, Susan saw that her face was drained of color. Her hair looked a mess. She tried to comb it into some semblance of order.

"Susan?" Paul's voice, strained, came from the other side of the door.

"I'm . . . all right." She opened the door and put her arms around his waist, resting her head on his shoulder. "I think I just had what they call a delayed reaction."

His mouth skimmed her hair. "Little wonder."

Her eyes met his. "You're tired too," she whispered, reaching up to smooth back his own mussed hair. "It's been quite a night, as another saying goes."

Paul chuckled. "Yes, it has. And now" — he took her hand to lead her across the bedroom — "it's time you got some sleep."

"But —" Susan stopped abruptly, her eyes drawn to the bed. The mattress was back in its proper place, covered with fresh sheets. The pillow was plumped. "Paul . . ."

"See, it's all ready for you." He guided her to sit down on the bed, though he remained standing. "No arguments. You sleep. I'll clean up."

She started to tell him she wouldn't think of it. He quickly stilled her protest with a finger on her lips.

"Good night," he whispered, bending to

remove her shoes. Smiling up at her, he said, "I'm afraid you'll have to take it from here."

Susan grinned back at him. "You're impossible." It was amazing how much better she felt. "Just one more favor," she asked, bringing her lips to his for a quick kiss. "There. Now I can sleep."

Paul seemed to have a hard time leaving her. Finally he turned to go. "I'll clean the living room first. If I get tired, I'll bunk on the sofa."

She shook her head. "Okay. Promise you'll get some sleep before the sun comes up."

Paul checked his watch. "That should be in about five and a half hours. I promise." He backed slowly away from her out of the room.

It was crazy, but Susan missed him already — and he was no more than twenty feet away. But she couldn't see him, and being able to see him was of extreme importance to her.

Still, exhaustion got the better of her after a few minutes. She didn't bother changing into a nightgown. Feeling safe and protected, she crawled under the fresh covers and immediately fell asleep.

Chapter Nine

Susan woke to the smell of frying bacon. At first, when she raised her head from the pillow, her stomach did a turn. She wondered if she would be sick again. But the feeling gradually passed and she realized she was just hungry.

From outside the bedroom came the sound of soft whistling. Paul was up. She conjectured he must be a morning person, one of the breed that bounces cheerily out of bed before sunrise.

Though she had a hard time rousing herself until well after ten, she wouldn't mind being wakened early if it meant having a fresh cup of coffee and your breakfast waiting for you — along with a kiss. The food and drink she could do without, but she was fast coming to realize that Paul's presence in her life was a needful thing.

With that inspiring thought, Susan threw back the covers and had no trouble at all getting up. Checking the time, she saw it was nearly ten. Paul hadn't come to waken her, and she was sure the reason she had slept so well was because of him. The temptation was great to rush out to the kitchen and give him a hug.

She shoved that enticing idea aside, but when her eyes focused on the place where her chest of drawers had laid, overturned, she saw it wasn't there. It had been set back in place. Looking around, she noted that everything that had been strewn on the floor was put away.

The tempting idea returned. Before she could act on it, she hurried into the bathroom and turned on the water full force. A quick shower and shampoo were in order first. Then she could give in to her impulses.

She emerged from the bedroom twenty minutes later, hair washed and combed. With clean slacks and her favorite knit sweater on, she went to the kitchen.

Susan found Paul just as she'd expected. He was standing by the stove, a piece of bread in one hand, a fork in the other. He dropped both when he saw her. She flung herself into his arms and whispered, "Good morning." Then she tilted her face up to receive his kiss.

"Mmm. It is," he responded fervently.

"And what a wonderful way to wake up,"

she murmured, inhaling deeply. "I love the smell of frying bacon."

"Your stomach is —"

"Fine," she assured him. "I also love the smell of your aftershave. How did you manage that?"

Paul gave her a slow smile. "I sneaked home. That is, after barricading your front door and borrowing the key to your back door."

She laughed. Not only had he shaved, his hair was neatly combed. He wore fresh jeans and a sweater similar to her own. "Where is home?" she asked.

"Not too far from here."

"I imagined you lived in an apartment near the office."

It was Paul's turn to laugh. "Hey, maybe I'm not so different than Rodney. I'm a beach bum on occasion too."

She didn't believe that, but her curiosity was aroused. "You live in one of the cottages along here?"

"On Briar Lane. You probably didn't notice it. The road's not clearly marked. It's a left turn off Quay Road about two miles out of town."

"That's interesting." She rested her hands on his arms. "By the way, you look like you're ready for a day on the water."

She glanced out the window and pronounced, "Sunny. All the clouds are gone. A light breeze. Great conditions for sailing."

"My gratitude for the weather report, and I wish I were going sailing . . . with you. But," he added solemnly, "we've got a couple of other things to do first."

She knew what he meant. Despite their delight in each other, the pending appointment with the sheriff wasn't far from their minds. Nor was the fate of Amy Lambert. She hated to consider what the law officer's response would be to her revelation that she'd spotted the child at Travers's lighthouse. Skepticism at best, she guessed. Outright scorn at worst.

There was something else on her mind. Hadn't she just told herself days ago that she had no intention of getting involved with any man in Gull Harbor? But now it had happened. She was in love and she had no power, nor wish, to fight it.

"You slept?"

Paul's question drew her attention.

"Yes. The more important question is, did you?"

"Enough," was all he said. "Would you like to eat inside or go out on the deck?"

"The deck."

She admired his profile as he poured coffee into mugs and arranged bacon and toast on plates that he took from the cupboard.

They went out on the deck and sat down together on the top step. Susan took a sip of her coffee. "This is good." Picking up a slice of bacon, she ate a bite. "Ditto for the food."

Paul grinned in response. "You've got a lot of talents," she added. Suddenly she realized how that sounded, but it was true.

"Maybe we could go shopping together sometime." He said it in an offhand way. "I've been told I'm pretty good at that too."

His remark triggered a connection in her mind. "Glendig's Market," she whispered.

"What?"

She touched his arm. "Paul, does the sheriff own Glendig's Market?"

He bit off a corner of his toast and chewed it. "No. The market's owned by his brother, Harold."

"Any other businesses in Gull Harbor with the family name?" She remembered her earlier thoughts on nepotism; it made her uneasy.

Paul cast a sideways glance at her. "Glendig's Garage. Another brother, Lou,

171

runs that one." He cleared his throat. "He'll have your tire fixed by the time you've met with Glen. I called him earlier."

Before she could reply, he went on, "Then there's the Higgins Agency."

Susan stopped in the midst of lifting a piece of toast to her mouth. "Higgins Agency?" She faced Paul. "That's run by a Glendig?"

"It used to be owned by a Harry Higgins," Paul said, meeting her eyes. "When he decided to retire to Arizona, he sold the business to Bill Glendig. You might have met Marion, the receptionist."

"Yes, I've had the pleasure." From Paul's smile, Susan knew he picked up on her distaste.

"Her sister, Helen, is married to Bill, so Marion's not directly related to the Glendig clan."

"Thank goodness."

"Not really. She's a Travers."

Susan almost dropped her coffee mug. "A Travers?"

"Daryl Travers is her brother."

Susan stared at Paul, astonished. But it made sense. Marion was no more hospitable than her brother.

"A penny for your thoughts," Paul

invited. When she didn't answer, he added, "No, make that a quarter."

Susan giggled, but more serious concerns spoiled her mood. "How about the *Beacon*? Is it backed by Glendig money?"

The look of relief on Paul's face was unmistakable. "It's owned by Ruth Westman's brother. He's a good man who doesn't try to influence his editor."

"I'm so glad."

"Me too," Paul whispered. He cupped her chin gently in his hand for a moment. "We'd better finish eating."

"Yes. But there's another thing. I don't remember hearing the name Glendig mentioned at Ruth's tea."

"That's not surprising. They aren't into teas and socials. The whole family breeds horses. That's their main interest, I understand."

"Oh." Susan picked up her last piece of bacon, then placed it back on her plate.

"What?" Paul coaxed, smoothing back a strand of her hair that had fallen over her cheek.

"I don't trust the sheriff. How can he give me a fair hearing when he and his brothers practically run Gull Harbor and . . . when he's indirectly related to the man who kidnapped Amy Lambert?"

"Susan, don't say that."

Paul's admonishment surprised her. "Why not? Isn't it true? You must believe yourself that the sheriff can't be impartial."

He shook his head. "I mean, we can't be sure that Travers kidnapped Amy and —"

Susan rose abruptly to her feet. Her eyes flashed with sudden anger. "What do you mean, we can't be sure Travers kidnapped Amy? I thought you believed me when I told you I saw the child in the window. You don't know how much courage it took for me to tell you that. Now you act as if I'm . . . crazy. I thought that you . . . that you . . ."

Dropping her plate on the step, she ran inside the cottage and slammed the door behind her. She was instantly ashamed, but she felt humiliated too. Tears stung her cheeks. "Don't cry!" she scolded herself, drawing her hands into tight fists.

The next thing she knew Paul was beside her. He turned her around so she had to look at him. His hands grasped her arms.

"You thought that I loved you," he finished for her, no trace of anger in his voice. "That's what you were about to say, wasn't it?"

She felt on fire; why was he embarrassing her this way? She refused to answer him.

"I do love you, Susan," he declared vehemently. "And if anyone's crazy around here, it's me. How could I love you this much when we barely know each other? I go to bed thinking of you, wake up thinking of you. I dream of you, of holding you, kissing you. I never want to hurt you." His gaze moved over her, finally focusing on her mouth. "I can't explain it, but I feel as if I've always known you."

Her lower lip quivered. How could she stay mad at him when he had just spilled his heart to her, when he was looking at her with such guilelessness? "Me, too," she confessed at last. "Everything you just said. . . ."

Her words were cut off as their lips met in a soulful kiss. Her hands at his back clutched the rough folds of his sweater. "You have to take inventory of your things before we meet with the sheriff," Paul reminded her in a shaky voice.

Yet they couldn't seem to let go of each other. "Don't doubt yourself, Susan, nor my faith in you."

She searched his eyes for a moment. "Then why did you say what you did about Travers?" The combative tone was gone from her voice. The kiss had taken care of that. But she felt confused.

Paul looked away from her. "Because . . . I can't stand to think that Amy might be a prisoner in the lighthouse, that Travers has held her there all this time." His hands slid from her waist to hold her hands. "I wouldn't turn my back on Travers for one minute. But why would he take a child? It doesn't make sense to me."

"For ransom money."

Paul looked doubtful. "Chris didn't have money, as far as I know."

"Her relatives?" Susan had a sudden idea. "Maybe that's why she left Gull Harbor. If there had been a ransom demand, she might have been too afraid to tell the authorities. Maybe she's following the kidnapper's orders." Susan knew her conjecture might be wishful thinking.

Paul appeared thoughtful. "I hadn't considered that," he said carefully. "We really have to go," he added in an apologetic tone.

Susan turned from him, letting the subject of Amy's kidnapping drop for the present. She would be talking with Sheriff Glendig about it soon enough.

Paul double-checked the barricaded door while she took inventory of her things and found nothing missing. Then she called Marion to inform her about the break-in. Marion coldly replied that the door would be replaced before evening.

The trip into town was uneventful. It gave Susan a chance to collect her thoughts. Still, the way Paul's hand held hers on the seat between them bore a deeper communication — the need for touch and reassurance on both their parts.

When they neared Bears' Tea Party, Susan glanced toward the window. She noticed the white bear was gone. Something else had taken its place — something that looked foreign in the shop window. "Slow down, Paul," she demanded, straining for a better view.

Obediently he put on the brakes. "What is it?"

"Bears' Tea Party is for sale!" She pointed at the large sign bearing the Higgins Agency name.

"For sale?" He almost brought the car to a stop, but a horn blared from behind and he kept moving.

Susan turned her head to look back. "Did you know that Anna was going to sell the shop?"

Paul glanced her way. "I had no idea. I

always thought Bears' Tea Party was her life."

"I got the same impression, especially when I saw her treat her bears like people."

Paul pulled into a parking space in front of the *Beacon* office. They got out of the car.

"Do you suppose Anna's having financial problems?" Susan continued as she went ahead of Paul into the office.

He ran a hand through his hair. "It's possible."

"I think I'll go by later and see her."

"Good idea," he replied as he stopped by his desk.

A clanking sound came from the back room. "Steven's still here." Paul grinned. "It seems that I wasn't the only one who didn't get much sleep last night."

Suddenly Susan felt ashamed. She hadn't even thanked him for all he'd done. "About last night, or I should say very early this morning, I never told you how much I appreciate your cleaning up the cottage and making breakfast."

When Paul turned to look at her, she went to him like a magnet and hugged him tight.

"I love the way you show your gratitude," he whispered, "but if I don't go back and check on Steven, he'll think I've gotten lost in the paperwork on my desk."

"We wouldn't want him to think that, would we?"

Paul looked mock serious. "Never. Why don't you come too?"

"Okay." She nearly forgot that the sheriff was due at the office in minutes. Maybe that was Paul's idea.

Steven met them with a smile, his hands and face smudged with ink. "She's up," he said with pride. He held out his hand. In his palm was a bolt that was broken in two. "This was the problem. Took me three hours to find it, but you can't argue with the replacement cost. Two dollars and fifty cents."

Paul picked up the bolt. "Terrific. So we're ready to print?"

Steven nodded. "I'm ready whenever you are." He sounded positive, but he appeared exhausted.

Paul put his arm around the pressman's shoulders. "Tell you what. You need some rest and I've got some work to do before we can print. So why don't you go home and rest a while. You can come back, say, around seven this evening."

Steven didn't argue. He excused himself to wash up. When he came back, Susan watched while Paul walked him to the door. It was obvious the two men had a good working relationship.

As Steven was going out, another man came in. It wasn't the sheriff, but it was Lou Glendig, the brother who owned the garage. After informing Susan that a nail had caused her flat tire, he let her know the repair was complete and that the cost would be ten dollars.

"Reasonable enough," she said as an aside to Paul as Lou left the office. "At least he didn't tell me I needed a new tire."

"Lou's an honest man." Paul paused. "I know you aren't impressed with his brother, but from what I've been able to judge, I believe the sheriff's doing the best job possible." He sounded adamant.

Susan felt her defenses rise again. She wished the subject of Sheriff Glendig hadn't become such a sore point between herself and Paul. Was she just being stubbornly judgmental?

Just then the person in question strode into the office, notebook in hand. Apparently all business, he didn't bother with any pleasantries. "What was it you wanted to talk to me about?" he asked, looking straight at Susan.

"Come on, why don't you sit down?"

Paul invited the sheriff before Susan could reply. He got the chair from beside his desk and placed it next to her desk.

The sheriff sat down on it and Susan took her own chair. Paul perched on the edge of her desk.

She felt Sheriff Glendig's eyes on her, expectant. Clearing her throat, she first told him that nothing was missing from her cottage as far as she could tell. Then she related her experience at Rocky Pointe, leaving out some of the details of her confrontation with Travers.

After she finished, the sheriff closed his notebook. "We'll check this out. But frankly, Susan, I don't expect to find any evidence that Amy Lambert has been a hostage in Travers's lighthouse."

Was that sarcasm in his tone of voice? Wasn't that what she had expected? "Thank you for your time, Sheriff Glendig." Her own voice sounded stiffly formal.

He gifted her with a slightly smug smile. "There is some news you might want to hear." When she only looked at him, the smile turned into a small frown. "Detective Osborn found a smudged fingerprint on the front door jamb of your cottage."

Susan sat erect. The sheriff smiled again. "I was sure you'd be interested. I can't promise that we'll make a positive I.D., though we're working on it."

"You'll let me know?"

"Of course." The sheriff rose from his chair. Paul eased himself off the desk. "I'll be back in touch soon," the law officer promised before turning to leave.

Paul accompanied Sheriff Glendig to the sidewalk outside the office. Susan couldn't hear their conversation. When Paul returned, he rested his hand on the back of her chair. "That wasn't so bad, was it?"

"Not too bad," she had to admit. "I still contend the sheriff doesn't believe me."

Paul sighed. "Try to trust him, just a little."

"All right. I'll try, Paul."

His fingers began to massage the nape of her neck. "You know what?" She shook her head, closing her eyes as he worked to ease the tension in her muscles. "Even if Sheriff Glendig is skeptical, you're convincing me more and more."

"Thank you, Paul," she said quietly. After a moment, she opened her eyes. "I have an idea. Why don't you come for breakfast tomorrow? My treat this time."

Paul's eyes crinkled. "Okay. And I'll hand deliver your copy of the *Beacon*."

Reluctantly Susan got up from her chair.

Paul's hand slid from her neck down her arm to her hand. His fingers intertwined with hers. It was getting to be a habit, she noticed, this lingering on both their parts.

They said their good-byes at the door and she went to her car. Occupied with her own thoughts, she almost forgot her intention to stop at Bears' Tea Party. The sight of the small shop as she pulled into the traffic on Main Street reminded her.

Susan swung into a parking space and walked up to the door. At least the OPEN sign was still posted. Inside, she saw a red-headed girl arranging bears on a shelf.

The girl stopped what she was doing and came over to her. "Hi. What can I help you with?"

Susan estimated the girl was about sixteen, though she was very tiny, almost frail-looking. "Is Anna in?" She glanced around the shop.

"Not today," the girl replied, regarding her curiously. "You know Anna?"

"Yes. We met not long ago. My name's Susan." She smiled. "I'm new to Gull Harbor."

"Oh." The girl smiled back shyly. "I'm Marcy."

"Nice to meet you, Marcy. I've been admiring Anna's bears. I thought I'd stop by and pick out one or two."

"We've got plenty to choose from."

"Yes, you do." Susan strolled over to a shelf and chose a bear wearing a green-and-white checkered vest. "I see Anna has the store up for sale," she said as casually as possible.

Marcy looked at her, wide-eyed. "Are you interested in buying the shop?"

Susan laughed. "No, I'm afraid I'm not much of a businesswoman." She put the bear back in its place and reached for another.

"That one just came in," Marcy offered.

"He's very handsome. Has Anna named him?"

"Not yet." Marcy fussed with the black jacket the bear wore.

"She really loves her animals, doesn't she?" Susan met Marcy's eyes. The girl looked sad.

"Yeah. I wish she didn't have to sell the place."

"Did she say why she has to?" Susan knew it was none of her business, but she sensed that Marcy wouldn't interpret her question as being snoopy.

"She didn't tell me, but Marion — she works at the Higgins Agency — came by the other day and had Anna sign some form," Marcy explained. "Probably a contract." The teenager shrugged.

The mention of Marion Travers's name made Susan instantly uncomfortable. She covered it by turning away from Marcy for a moment to take a third bear from the shelf. "I hope Anna's reason for selling isn't because business is bad."

"I don't think so." Marcy smiled. "Would you like that one?" She indicated the bear.

"Yes, and this one too." Susan again picked out the bear with the checkered vest. She handed the two animals to Marcy, following the girl to the cash register.

Marcy rang up the sale. "The total's seventy dollars."

"That'll about break my budget." Susan silently scolded herself for not checking the price tags first.

"Anna should be in on Friday," Marcy volunteered. "You could stop back then."

"Thank you. I'll plan to do that." Susan took her purchases from the teenager and started on her way. At the door, she turned to look back. Her eyes swept over the cozy little shop. Though every nook and corner was crammed with bears, the place seemed empty without Anna's presence.

Chapter Ten

Susan went to bed right after supper that evening. With autumn fast approaching, the days were getting noticeably shorter. It was already dark outside when she crawled under the covers, but there was a full moon. Its light cast lacy patterns on the floor of the room.

As Susan set her alarm, she wondered if she would dream that night. Her thoughts lately had been so troubled, though there had been some happy ones too. It was those happy ones she tried to concentrate on.

Instead, the image of Amy's face at the lighthouse window played in her mind like some movie reel stuck on fast forward and reverse. Susan desperately wished there were a way for her to rescue the child and learn whether the key to Amy's disappearance lay with the man who acted as if he had a quarrel with the whole world.

She considered the enigma that was Daryl Travers. Had he always carried a chip on his shoulder? Or had something happened to him that had embittered him so that he felt it was his duty to bully others?

Maybe she would ask Paul those questions, though she had a suspicion he couldn't tell her much. He wasn't a native of the area. No doubt his encounters with Travers had been minimal, if unpleasant. But he did know enough to warn her in no uncertain terms to stay away from Rocky Pointe. And she hadn't listened.

Somewhere in the midst of her search for answers, Susan drifted off to sleep. When her eyes flew open hours later, she could have sworn that what had wakened her was real, not imagined.

She had heard crying, the loud, plaintive wailing of a child. The child's face was immersed in shadow, yet she recognized it instantly. Or did she?

"Joey!" The word was half formed, more a moan. Susan shook her head. *No. The child wasn't Joey.* "Amy," she said under her breath as she groped her way out of bed.

The moonlight was gone from her room. Only the red glow of the numbers on her new digital clock loaned a hint of illumination to her surroundings. She'd bought the clock on impulse after leaving Bears' Tea

Party, reasoning that she needed an alarm to guarantee she didn't oversleep the next morning.

She read the numerals. Three o'clock. It would be hours yet before dawn.

Susan made her way slowly over to the window. Hugging her sides, she peered through the glass into the blackness. Since she'd learned of Amy's abduction, the cottage had taken on a certain forlornness for her. But she hadn't realized until the break-in just how desolate the place could seem in the middle of the night.

Nerves already strained, she listened for any sound. Had her mind interpreted another signal as crying? A shiver passed through her. What if the person or persons who had broken into her cottage had come back?

As quickly as she could in the dark, she made a round through the various rooms, stopping to peek out every window. She saw nothing, heard nothing but the muffled beat of waves breaking against the shore. Even the wind had died to a whisper.

She tested the back door that she had locked earlier. The dead bolt was still set. The front door had been replaced, complete with a brand-new lock, though she considered that Paul's barricade could have deterred a small army, if necessary. Her safety appeared secure.

She might be safe, but what about Amy? Just what was it the sheriff intended to do with the information she'd given him?

With a sigh, Susan crept back to bed and crawled under the covers again. At that moment, it seemed she had never felt so utterly alone.

When Paul arrived in the morning, he had some disappointing news. "We had another minor problem with the beast," he told Susan, following her into the kitchen.

"Oh, no." She felt a little let down, but more sorry for Paul.

"Not to worry." He came to stand beside her. "It's fixed now, and Steven was about to start printing when I left the office. It does mean, though, that I'll have to bring by your copy of the *Beacon* later this afternoon, if that's okay."

"It's more than okay," she said, noting the color in his cheeks at her reply. He looked rested, but she had to ask, "Were you at the office all night?"

"No. I went home when Steven came in. He called me later to tell me the press was down. But what is this?" He tilted her face up and ran his fingers lightly along the hollows beneath her eyes.

She busied herself pouring juice into two glasses. But she knew what he meant. Though she'd applied extra concealer above her cheekbones, no amount of makeup could hide the physical evidence of her weariness.

"Didn't you sleep, Susan?"

She looked at Paul. "For a while. I woke up about three. That is, something woke me. It must have been a dream. I . . . think."

He frowned. "A bad dream?"

"I thought someone was crying, Paul. A child. Amy," she added hoarsely.

"Susan." He immediately came and took her into his arms.

She rested her cheek against his sweater and heard the thudding of his heart, his even breathing. They were sounds she could have drawn solace from earlier. "I went through the cottage," she explained, "checking the doors and windows. I didn't find anything, of course. But I'm not convinced it was only a dream."

Paul drew back a little. Framing her face in his hands, he said, "I'll stop by Sheriff Glendig's office this afternoon and find out what I can."

"Thank you," she said softly.

"I wouldn't get my hopes up," he cautioned, as if reading her mind. "I doubt he'll have very much to tell us yet."

"I suppose not, but it's so hard waiting."

"I know." He held her tight for a moment. "Have faith, Susan. Believe that Amy will be found, safe and well."

"I'll try," she said at last. Moving out of his arms, she took plates from the cupboard. "Our breakfast is getting cold."

Paul watched as she arranged the omelets that she'd made onto the dishes. She handed him a plate and they carried their breakfast out to the deck again. Though the air was brisk, the sky was cloudless and there was an inviting warmth to the sun.

Paul brought a forkful of eggs to his mouth. "This is the best omelet I've ever eaten," he declared after swallowing the bite.

Susan smiled at his compliment, even if he might be exaggerating a bit.

While they ate, they watched the water. There was a lone sailboat some distance out. Briefly Susan wondered whether it might be the *Silver Belle*.

When she saw that Paul had finished eating, she asked, "Can you stay a while?"

"There's nothing I'd enjoy more than spending the day with you, Susan." His eyes moved to her lips and stayed there for a couple of heartbeats. "Unfortunately I've got to make several phone calls and start work on next week's edition of the *Beacon.*"

"That reminds me, will I have an assignment?"

Paul grinned at her. "How does a joint assignment sound?"

"You mean. . . ."

"The two of us, yes."

"That sounds most intriguing."

"I was hoping you'd think so." Paul beamed. "Our next issue should be mostly filler, unless there's a breaking story." He left unsaid between them what that breaking story might be. "But on Monday, there'll be an all-day mayors' conference, held in Pitston Bay, incidentally."

Her reaction must have satisfied him, for he went on. "A meeting that important requires more diligent coverage than usual, don't you agree?"

"Much more." Susan was already delighted at the prospect.

Paul rose to go. She walked him to his car. "Thank you for the most fantastic breakfast of my life," he said, leaning against the car door.

"It seems we've formed a culinary mutual admiration society."

"Mmm. It seems we have. But there's much more to admire about you than that. I forgot to tell you, Susan. Your articles on the rally and tea were letter perfect. The rally is this issue's lead story."

"Really?"

"Uh-huh. Remember you told me you thought I had many talents?" She nodded. "Well, my talents are nothing compared to yours."

Their lips came together as he pulled her into his embrace. They lingered in the kiss until finally he drew back. Their partings were definitely not getting easier, Susan decided with a sigh, and if Paul kept flattering her like this, she would soon agree to cover a tarantula race in the middle of the tropics if he asked her to.

He got into his car and rolled down the window to tell her to expect him sometime after four. She waited while he drove off. Then she went back inside the cottage, pondering what to do with herself the next several hours.

When Paul returned with her paper, Susan realized she was more eager to hear about his conversation with Sheriff Glendig than to see her write-ups on the rally and tea.

"So, what did the sheriff have to say?" she asked, unable to keep the wistfulness from her voice.

Paul led her to the sofa. They sat down together. "First," he said, placing the *Beacon* in her lap, "look at this." He unfolded the paper and pointed to her article on the rally.

She looked it over and was pleased with the layout of the piece as well as the star billing Paul had given her. His own tiny two paragraphs on the no-show developer's rally had been relegated to the bottom of the page.

Paul next showed her the spread on the social. "The pictures came out well, don't you think?"

Perusing them, Susan had to agree.

"In those six photos, you managed to capture the faces of all the women who attended the tea."

She looked at Paul, incredulous. "How did you determine that?"

He smiled. "I know the faces of almost everyone in Gull Harbor, and I've made a special effort to acquaint myself with the ladies who attend Ruth Westman's teas.

Let's say I have a vested interest in the event."

Susan remembered that he had told her the newspaper was owned by Ruth's brother.

Paul put the paper aside and took her hands in his.

"About your meeting with the sheriff?" she asked, almost dreading the answer.

His face grew somber. "The sheriff and Detective Osborn paid a visit to Travers this morning."

"And?"

He shook his head. "Nothing. Susan, they didn't find Amy at the lighthouse."

"No, of course they didn't," she retorted before he could say more. "Did they go there expecting Travers to just hand the child over?" She withdrew her hands from Paul's and rose suddenly from the sofa.

"Oh, good morning, Sheriff Glendig," she began with mock solicitousness. "I'm so glad to see you and Detective Osborn. In fact, I've been expecting you." She folded her hands together and gave a small bow. "You've come for Amy, have you?"

Hardly caring what Paul thought of her charade, she continued. "Please come in, sheriff. And you, too, detective. I apologize for the condition of the place. There are a few broken windows, makes the rooms a little drafty. And there's not much furniture, just an old sofa and a mattress to sleep on." Her words dripped with mock humility.

Hurrying on, she said, "But I assure you that Amy's been well taken care of. I've brought her toys, some dolls and bears. Of course she misses her mother. She cries and I've had to hit her a few times to make her behave. But what are you going to do? I mean, you've got to . . ." Susan broke off in a sob.

Instantly Paul was at her side. "Stop it, Susan! Stop torturing yourself like this."

"Torturing *myself?*" She twisted away from him when he tried to hold her. "What about Amy?" she cried. "Are Sheriff Glendig and his detective the judge and jury of what happened to her?"

"The verdict is still out," he shot back.

"Is it, Paul?" She faced him defiantly. "I thought the sheriff made it very clear that he blamed Amy's disappearance on one man — Sean Lambert. His mind is closed. He doesn't believe that I saw Amy in that window. No one does," she said icily, aware that her indictment included the man she loved.

That man was maddeningly persistent.

He took her by the shoulders; his eyes were dark with anger. "I've already told you I believe you. Do you think I would lie to you, Susan?"

"Then help me." She gripped his arms, and he winced as her fingernails dug into his flesh. But she couldn't stop herself. She needed him to listen to her, to tell her he would do anything she asked of him because he loved her.

"We can go back to Rocky Pointe, Paul. We'll go after sunset. We can camp out. I have a lens for nighttime photography. Since the sheriff at least questioned him, Travers is bound to make a move. If we're there just at the right time, if we're patient. . . ." She stopped, out of breath from her impassioned plea.

"No, Susan!" Paul caught her hands, deliberately lowering them to her sides. "I do know how you feel. But we can't go snooping around Travers's property, taking foolish chances on some vague hope."

"It may be a vague hope to you, Paul Stuart," she snapped. "But it might be the only one Amy's got. Think of that."

He shook his head. "No. It's not the way. Let the authorities follow up. The sheriff's given me his assurance that he'll do everything possible. The investigation's not finished."

"Amy's life might end before the investigation does."

Paul looked away, shoulders slumped. "Susan, you know that I love you . . . desperately," he said in a near whisper.

Susan's hands began to tremble. Emotion choked the words she wanted to say. "Please just go, Paul," she said at last, yearning to tell him that she loved him too. She felt ashamed, but she was also angry and disappointed in him. Had she been a fool to fall for a man who, to use his own words, she barely knew?

Their eyes met for a long moment, then he turned to leave. Susan stood still where she was, but she couldn't stop herself from watching him. At the front door, he hesitated, looking back briefly. The hurt was all there, like a fresh wound, between them. "I love you," he said simply, then left before she could reply.

Susan sagged against the door. Closing her eyes, she clung to his last words. But his love for her, hers for him, couldn't change the decision she'd already made. If Paul wouldn't go with her to Rocky Pointe, she would go alone. Tonight.

Like someone in a trance, she went over

to the sofa and sat down. The neatly folded copy of the *Beacon* lay beside her. Mechanically she picked it up and turned to the inside page. Though she didn't understand why, her eyes were drawn to the Closet Poet's column. This week's poem was titled "New Love." Again, it was by K. Garnett.

She felt compelled to read it. She hadn't gone more than two lines before she knew this poem was far different than the one she'd read the week before. "New Love" was more lyrical, more intimate. Far more intimate.

The poem spoke to her heart and sent her emotions reeling. By the time she finished, she realized the lines had been written for her. She read the last stanza again:

We watched the sunset gild the foam
and small waves nibble at the shore;
Sometime between the last gull's flight
and moonrise
I heard your love, singing to me softly.

Susan hugged the paper to her breast as a tear slipped down her cheek. Her anger was gone. In its place melancholy settled over her like fog on a wasted shore. Would those sentiments in the poem ever come true now? Could her doubts be overcome by love?

Chapter Eleven

It was well after dark when Susan left her cottage. She used the moon for light to make her way down the beach to the marina. Bypassing the building, she went straight to where the *Anne Marie* was docked. She had no desire to explain to Sam why she was taking the boat out at such a late hour.

Placing her knapsack in the bow of the *Anne Marie*, she mentally reviewed the supplies she had brought along: Binoculars, camera fitted with film and a night-time lens, swamp waders, a small flashlight, coffee, a pair of wire cutters.

Wire cutters. Just the idea that she'd actually gone into town after supper and bought them made her nervous. What did she expect to use them for?

Travers's fence was barbed wire. She couldn't climb it. If the place looked absolutely deserted, she might be emboldened to take out a little piece of that fence. After all, she was desperate to find proof of

Amy's captivity. Was trespassing too high a price to pay?

Susan knew the answer and it prompted her to get on with her plans. She scanned the water. There was a light chop to the surface. It hardly disturbed the silvery seascape created by moon and ocean. On another night and under different circumstances, she would have declared the setting romantic.

But there was no romance in the task that lay ahead of her. She expected her wait at the lighthouse to be tedious and uncomfortable. Though she had worn both a sweater and her warmest jacket, the air was brisk with the kind of chill that no amount of clothing could ward off.

Susan looked back at the marina. For an instant, she thought she saw movement at one of the windows and wondered if it was Sam. Praying that if it was, he hadn't seen her, she hurried to climb aboard the *Anne Marie*. Then she froze in mid-step.

Something told her that she wasn't alone. A tremor went through her. It couldn't be Sam, could it?

"Susan!"

She let out a cry, whirling to face the man whom she had imagined to be an adversary. "Paul!" She gasped.

He made a move toward her, then stopped no more than ten feet away. "I scared you. I'm sorry." Though his face was concealed from her by shadows, there was no mistaking his voice, his build, his stance.

Her initial shock at seeing him there wore off, replaced by sudden anger — and something else. Was it fear? "What are you doing here?" she demanded, cringing at the harsh tone of her own voice. But she couldn't let him think she was glad he'd come, not when his purpose must be to dissuade her from her plans.

"Susan."

His voice caressed her name in a way that made her bones feel as if they were melting. Wasn't that just what he wanted? For her to throw herself into his arms and tell him that he was right and she was wrong?

She wasn't sure how well he could see her, but she set her jaw defiantly. "I'm on my way and you're not going to change my mind."

"I know that," he said softly.

To her disgust, instead of getting into the boat, she took a step in his direction. "Why did you come, Paul?"

"Because you were determined. You

wouldn't listen to me, to reason."

"But *reason* is doing everything possible to help an innocent child," she rejoined. Still, her feet seemed to have ideas of their own. A few more steps and she was face-to-face with Paul. His features were clearly visible now in the moonlight, but his eyes were veiled. She couldn't read them. "You can't stop me, Paul." She meant it as a warning. How he might try to stop her — or how she would resist — she hadn't a clue.

"I have no intention of that. I'm going with you."

"Going with me?" she echoed.

"Yes, and we'd better be on our way. It's already after nine." He took hold of her hand to lead her back to the *Anne Marie*.

Susan followed without resistance. "You were waiting for me?"

Paul turned to her, smiling. "Since about seven." He surprised her with a kiss, silencing any reply.

Together they climbed into the boat and he started the motor.

"Don't you think we should use the sails?" she asked. She didn't mention that Travers wasn't the only one she didn't want to hear the sound of a motor.

"Just when we get near Rocky Pointe,"

Paul replied, hoisting the anchor.

Susan hugged her knees and watched as he steered the *Anne Marie* away from the dock.

Once they were out on open water, he motioned for her to sit beside him in the stern. When she did, he put his arm around her.

"Thank you for coming, Paul."

His breath warmed her cheek. "I couldn't let you go alone."

At that moment, she almost told him she loved him, almost turned to kiss him. But this wasn't the time for them to toss caution aside and get lost in each other. So she contented herself with snuggling against him while he guided the *Anne Marie* toward their goal.

Paul cut the motor a couple of miles out from Rocky Pointe. Clouds partially hid the moon, and there was just enough illumination to make out the shadowy presence of the lighthouse and keeper's quarters.

Susan helped him set the sails, then he maneuvered the boat into a small cove where it wouldn't be visible from Travers's property. He got out first, taking her hand.

"Wait, Paul." She retrieved her knapsack and unzipped it.

"What?" he whispered.

She held up her swamp waders where he could see them. "I have to put these on," she whispered back.

"Okay."

"Where are yours?" Susan squinted at his feet; he wore what appeared to be hiking boots.

"I'll have to buy a pair."

"You'd look cute in them," she said, voice still hushed.

"Not nearly as cute as you, Susan."

Faces close, she asked, "Why are we whispering?"

"It's more romantic?" He said it aloud, but barely.

His answer deserved an appropriate response. She reached to press a kiss on his lips, then pulled away, careful not to let the feelings between them ignite further. Turning from Paul, she slipped into her waders.

They climbed the rocks side by side, picking their way across the slimy surfaces. Where the path narrowed, Paul went on ahead.

Just below Travers's fence, they stopped. Susan took out her binoculars. Searching the water, she was shocked to detect something moving on the waves. Unsure, she handed the glasses to Paul. "What do you see?"

He looked through them. "A boat," he said finally. "I hear it too."

She listened. There was the faint drone of a motor. "Is it headed this way?"

"Can't tell yet."

The next instant a blinding flash of light arced across the sky above the water. Instinctively Susan dropped to her knees. Paul did the same. They huddled against each other. "What was that?" she asked shakily, wanting to believe it was an approaching storm.

Before he could reply, the light shone again. It definitely wasn't a thunderstorm. "The lighthouse!" they exclaimed together. Paul trained the binoculars on the tower.

"Do you see anything?"

"No." He handed the binoculars back to her.

She focused them on the water below. The boat they'd spotted was approaching the shore. In another beam of light from the tower, she saw the name on its stern. "*Mach III*," she announced, like some message of doom.

"*Mach III*?"

She met Paul's eyes, wishing she could read the expression on his face. "When I was heading back to the marina from Barr Estuary last week, some guys in a ketch made a few passes at the *Anne Marie*." She tried to sound casual.

"A few passes at you," he replied, not fooled.

"Yes." Pausing, she added, "That's their boat. The *Mach III*. I wonder what they're doing here."

"I don't know, but if we stick around, we're bound to find out." Paul grabbed her hand. "Come on," he urged.

She followed him to a place by the fence where a large clump of bramble bushes grew. They would offer concealment.

It didn't take long for the *Mach III* to pull up to the base of the rocks. Susan and Paul took turns watching as the men dropped anchor. There were three of them; Susan surmised they were the same men who had circled her boat. They started up what appeared to be a set of stone steps.

"Where've you been? You're an hour late!"

Susan clamped her hand over her mouth to stifle a gasp of astonishment. She felt Paul's arm come around her protectively. "Travers," he pronounced. Though she couldn't see where Travers was standing, identification was unnecessary.

"Everything's cool, boss," one of the men yelled up from below.

"Get a move on," Travers roared back, "or you'll be cooling your heels in cement shoes custom-made by Torvino."

The men didn't reply, but the implications of Travers's threat gave Susan a chill.

Paul took the binoculars. "Look, Susan. Right there." He pointed, giving her the glasses again.

The hulking outline of a man came into dim focus. She knew it was Travers. He was standing just outside his fence, facing the ocean. The men came up to him.

"Since you clowns weren't around, I had to get everything ready myself." He motioned for the men to follow him. They went through what seemed to be a gate and disappeared out of sight.

Susan lowered the binoculars. "What do we do now?"

"Wait," Paul whispered into her ear.

They waited and watched, though there was nothing to see, not even a light visible from inside the tower or the keeper's quarters. The wind was stronger, almost frigid, on the promontory; the bushes rattled with every gust.

Susan brought out the thermos of coffee she'd packed. She and Paul shared two cups of the hot brew. What talking they did was about inconsequential matters. She sensed neither of them could bear to bring up the subject that consumed their minds — the fate of Amy Lambert and what Travers and the others were doing inside the lighthouse.

Finally, after what might have been an hour, the men emerged. As they came into plainer view, Paul crouched on his hands and knees and crept forward to an opening in the undergrowth.

"Where are you going?" Susan whispered, inching along right behind him.

"To take pictures," he said softly over his shoulder. "Let me have your camera."

She got the camera from her knapsack and gave it to Paul. Keeping close, she followed him out from the undergrowth. Thorns pricked her face; she winced in pain. Still hidden by the darkness, they were within yards now of Travers and his men.

Peering around Paul, she saw that two of the men were carrying something between them that looked like an oblong box.

"How much is Torvino paying for this lot?" one of them asked.

"Enough, Rivera," Travers said tersely.

"What about the other problem, boss?"

the second man put in.

"And what'd I just tell you a little while ago about asking questions?" Travers demanded. "It's been taken care of," he added coldly.

Other problem. Taken care of. Susan stiffened, an image of the face in the window burning in her mind. She wasn't even aware that Paul had gone forward again. Not until she heard the terrible crack of something under his foot. It could have been a gunshot, but it wasn't. A fallen branch, no doubt, from one of the bushes. But it was enough.

One of the men cursed.

"What was that?" Travers roared.

"Go back, Susan!"

Dimly Susan heard Paul's urgent order. She didn't obey it.

The next second they were both caught in a beam of light like deer in a hunter's headlights. And like deer, they froze.

"Well, if it ain't the editor of our local rag and his little lady reporter." The taunt was Travers's. "Pulling night duty, are we?"

"Run, Susan!"

Paul shoved her away from the light. This time, swallowed for an instant by the darkness, she made her feet move.

She might have somehow managed to escape through the maze of tangled undergrowth. But she couldn't keep herself from looking back. When she did, she saw Travers punch Paul in the stomach.

"No!" she shouted, stumbling in her haste to reach the man she loved.

He was bent double, clutching his middle. "Go," he moaned. "Please go, Susan!"

Agony was written on Paul's face. Yet he turned again to Travers. She saw his valiant try to save himself — and her.

His attempted punches were deflected by Travers's greater strength. The other men joined the fray. She watched in horror as Rivera delivered a glancing blow to Paul's head. He staggered toward her. She began to reach for him, then something urged her to take other action. Was it the terrible pain in his eyes? Or his plea that she forgive him?

She had no idea she could mobilize herself so quickly as her legs began to carry her in earnest down the steep rocks. She didn't look around; she didn't need to.

The men were right behind her. They called to her, jeering. Her feet flew faster, the waders hardly making contact with the slippery ground.

It was a noble effort on her part. In the end, it wasn't enough. Travers caught up to her first. She felt his hot breath on her neck as his hand clamped down on her arm.

He jerked her backward. She reacted by kicking his shin. Vile words spewed from his mouth as his grip on her loosened.

Frantically she tried to gain purchase again on the slick rocks. She couldn't. There was nothing to hold onto, only the sensation of falling. She put her hands out to brace herself. It wasn't enough.

Raucous laughter filled her ears, sickening her. Desperately she sought a way to fool the men. Just before they reached her, an idea came to mind. Against every instinct she had to fight their efforts to take her captive, she closed her eyes and made herself go limp.

Chapter Twelve

"Hey, boss. The little lady's out too."

Rivera's voice close by her ear told Susan that he had reached her first. She detected the odor of alcohol on his breath. It made her shudder inwardly. With all the will-power she could summon, she forced herself to lie still.

But her heart was pumping furiously in her chest, and she had to keep telling herself to relax. Her one chance to save Paul and herself hinged on her ability to fool Travers and his men.

Her waders were roughly pulled off, and hands grabbed hold of her ankles. She knew the hands were Travers's when he spoke.

"We'll haul Sleeping Beauty and her prince inside. For now," he added.

His remark drew guffaws from the other men. Then Rivera said, "We gonna tie them up, boss?"

"No. We're going to let them go fancy-free."

Travers's biting sarcasm wasn't lost on Susan, though she doubted Rivera even noticed it. He appeared too much in awe of his "boss."

Susan felt herself being carried back up the rocks. There was the creaking sound of a door swinging on its hinges. A strong, moldy smell burned her nostrils and she braved opening her eyes a sliver. The men had entered the lighthouse.

A faint trickle of light was coming from somewhere, though it did little good. She could vaguely see Travers's form; his face was concealed in darkness.

Footsteps sounded behind her. They had to belong to the other men. No doubt they were carrying Paul in. She desperately needed to hear his assurance that he was all right. She feared he was badly hurt.

Can't think of that, she told herself. She must not think of anything but finding a way to outwit Travers. Hadn't Paul been strong for her when her cottage had been broken into? It was her turn to be strong for him — for them both.

Susan heard another door open and shut after them. Then she felt herself being lowered. Travers and Rivera let her go and she fell against cold wood. A splinter jagged her palm. She automatically winced — and prayed the men hadn't noticed.

They must not have. "Put him down there," Travers barked.

She heard a muffled thud close by and knew Paul had been dropped to the floor too. At least he was near. It was more than she'd dared hope for.

There was light in the room. She was aware of its brightness even with her eyes shut.

"Tie their hands and feet." Travers gave the order.

The men didn't bother to take off her jacket. They grabbed her arms and jerked them behind her back, tying her wrists with thick cord. Then they bound her ankles in the same manner.

A hand gripped Susan's shoulder. Alcohol-laced breath hit her face. "When are you going to wake up, Sleeping Beauty?" Travers taunted. Huge fingers pushed back a lock of her hair from her forehead.

Revulsion knifed through her. She wanted to revile Travers as the scum that he was. But her mouth was as dry as parched dune grass. Sheer terror made her continue to feign unconsciousness.

"So what are we going to do with them?" another voice asked in an agitated tone. It was the man Susan considered might be more reasonable than the others.

After a silence, Travers said finally, "We'll have to get rid of them. You know that, Sully."

"Get rid of them? Gee, do we have to do that, boss?"

Sully's questions sounded almost innocent. If only he were the boss, not Travers, Susan thought that she and Paul might have a chance.

"Don't go mushy on me." Travers's voice was brittle. "You know how this thing plays."

Is that how it had been with the child? The possibility that Amy had met such a fate was too horrifying for Susan to consider.

"When?" Rivera put in.

Susan heard the men move away from her. She opened her eyes a bit again. Travers and the others were standing several feet away. She made out a table; they were standing around it. A lamp of some sort, perhaps a kerosene lantern, was set on the table. It was the light source she'd detected.

She didn't care at that moment to examine her surroundings. Her concern was for Paul. Cautiously she turned her head toward him. Her eyes quickly swept over him. She didn't like what she saw.

His eyes were closed. He could have been sleeping peacefully, except that his face was ghostly pale and his forehead was streaked with what appeared to be dried blood.

Paul's jacket was still on, but his glasses were missing, no doubt knocked off during the scuffle. Susan yearned to ease his suffering. Then it occurred to her that he wasn't hurting at the moment. He really was unconscious, not playacting as she was.

That knowledge triggered other worries. What would happen when he woke up? She wouldn't allow herself to think if. She doubted he would be in any condition to try to escape if Travers slipped up and gave them that chance. Would Paul even remember what had happened just before Rivera struck him? Or would he have amnesia?

Susan sucked in a sharp breath at the sudden idea that train of thought gave her. The noise caused her to panic. Had the men heard her stirring?

Forcing her eyes closed except for a crack, she waited, nerves frayed. No one seemed to be paying any attention to her. Travers and Rivera were in a heated discussion about something. It took her a minute to realize that the subject was cement shoes for her and Paul.

"Okay, let's get the rest of that load ready," Travers said.

"And let our prisoners get their beauty rest," Sully added to the sound of chuckles.

Shoes shuffling and scraping on the bare floor told Susan the men were going out. She wished they would leave the lantern behind.

They didn't. Yet she had her wish fulfilled in a different way. After she was sure the men had gone, she opened her eyes wide and saw the room was partially illumined by a strong, if narrow, shaft of moonlight. It cut directly across the area where Paul lay.

As her eyes adjusted, she could make out other things. Besides the table, there was a sofa in the middle of the room. A desk took up one corner.

A sense of urgency drove Susan to action. There was no telling when the enemy would return, but she believed Travers wouldn't leave her and Paul alone for long.

Testing her bonds, Susan tried to move her hands. The rope chafed painfully at her

218

wrists. The knot had been tied with a bit of slack, but not enough for her to work her hands loose. She needed Paul's help.

At least she wasn't shackled to a chair or post, she consoled herself. Apparently neither was Paul. Imitating the movement of a bushy-backed sea slug, she inched her way over to him.

He was slumped forward slightly, chin resting on his chest. His breathing was even, not labored, and that gave her hope that she might be able to wake him. Teetering a little, she leaned close and pressed her lips to his cheek. It felt cool. "I love you," she whispered. Then in a louder voice, she said, "Paul?"

He didn't answer, but she hadn't expected him to. She called his name again and his head moved slightly. Drawing encouragement from the brief response, she nudged him with her shoulder, then blew on his face. When that didn't rouse him, she pushed him so hard that he almost toppled over.

He let out a soft moan.

"Paul! Wake up. Please wake up!"

He moaned a second time. She thought she saw his eyelids flutter. The next instant they opened partially.

"Paul! Can you hear me? It's Susan!"

The words, full of urgency, echoed through the room. Susan imagined that Travers was outside. She held her breath, expecting to hear the sound of his boots. Instead, she heard Paul speak her name.

He said it once more and her heartbeat quickened. Though his voice sounded thready, he had formed a coherent word. But his eyes were glazed with pain. It was his next words that brought tears to her own eyes.

"I love you," he said in a hoarse whisper.

"I love you too, Paul. Very much."

He tried to sit up straighter, but couldn't. "My head hurts." He groaned softly. "Where are we?"

"In Travers's lighthouse."

"Travers's lighthouse?"

"Do you remember we came here looking for Amy? We were just outside Travers's fence when he and his men found us. You tried to fight them off, but one of them hit you and knocked you unconscious."

"That's what happened?" He looked confused.

"Yes. They took us captive."

"My . . . hands are tied," he said, dazed.

"Mine are too. Paul . . ." Susan brought her face as close to his as possible. There was no delicate way she could say what she had to. "Travers plans to kill us." Paul's only response was a sucked-in breath. Was he alert enough to grasp the bleakness of their situation? If he wasn't, she would have to make him understand. "We've got to get out of here. Travers and his men are gone now, but they could come back any second."

"Yes . . . get out of here. I . . . Susan, I can hardly see you. My glasses . . ."

"Your glasses must have fallen off outside. But there's no time to worry about that now. Could you help me, please? Try to untie my hands." She turned her back to him. "Turn your back too," she ordered. He hesitated, then obeyed. Her hands groped for his and found them. His fingers fumbled at the rope binding her wrists.

"The knot is on the other side, Paul."

He fumbled some more, but finally his fingers tightened around the knot. She felt the rope begin to slacken as he tugged at it.

"I'm sorry," he said quietly.

"Sorry? Why? You're getting it."

"No. Not about that. I'm sorry I failed you."

"Don't say that! You didn't fail me." Earnestness strained her voice. "It wasn't your idea to come back to the lighthouse. You tried to tell me how dangerous Travers was. I didn't want to listen."

"No, but I know why you felt you had to come back. If I was the man I should be, I could have fought him and the others off so that you'd get away."

"You're all the man I could ever want." Her trembling words momentarily stopped his progress on the knot as he turned just enough to bury his face in her hair. Then he set to work feverishly and the cord soon came loose from her wrists.

"You did it, Paul!" She felt not only the warmth of his presence at her back but a small surge of triumph. "Now let me free you."

She made surprisingly short work of untying him. His arms came immediately around her and they clung to each other as she soothed the angry cut on his forehead with kisses. "Does it hurt?" she asked.

"Not anymore," he whispered. Reluctantly he released her, but not before he'd told her all over again how much he loved her. Then he bent to free her ankles.

She stood up gingerly while Paul finished untying his own ankles. "Can you stand?"

He was silent a moment. "I . . . don't know."

She reached for his hands, urging him, "We have to hurry."

Paul tried twice before he was able to get up from the floor. "I'm pretty dizzy," he confessed, sagging against her.

"It's no wonder, but we can't stay here. I'll help you." Secretly she was worried that he had a concussion. She promised herself that as soon as they reached safety, she would make him see a doctor.

"I'm ready," he said, shifting his weight so that he didn't lean too heavily on her.

Almost pulling him along, she started for the door. When she tried to turn the knob, it wouldn't budge. "The door's locked," she announced, realizing how foolish she'd been to think otherwise. "We'll have to go out the window."

"There's another problem, Susan."

"What is it?" Could she handle any more?

"We don't have our shoes, or in your case, your waders."

She had to laugh at his observation, both out of sheer relief that his mind was working more clearly than she'd thought and because in her own preoccupation with their escape, she hadn't bothered to notice they were only wearing their socks. "So we'll have to find them."

"Why don't we see if we can get some more light in here?"

"Good idea." Susan went over to the window and yanked on the curtain. It came open and moonlight flooded the room, brightening every spot except the corners. Her eyes frantically scanned the room for their foot gear. They picked out a dark shape on the sofa. She went over to it and discovered that it was her knapsack.

Her toe hit something. She picked up the offending object. "It's one of your shoes, Paul." She found the other one close by. "I've got both of them," she amended.

He came up beside her. "You were supposed to let me help you walk," she accused gently as she gave him his shoes.

His hand rested on her shoulder. "Your help is deeply appreciated, but I feel better now."

She wasn't sure if he was being truthful, but at least he seemed able to navigate on his own. While he put on his shoes, she continued the search for her waders. She didn't find them.

"You need your waders. The rocks are going to be slippery," he argued.

"I'll be all right. We can't waste another minute."

"Then you're wearing these." He took off his shoes and gave them back to her.

"No. You need them. Besides, they won't fit me."

"I'll manage without them. And they'll fit you well enough." He effectively blocked any further argument by kneeling in front of her and slipping the shoes onto her feet.

They weren't as sloppy on her as she would have imagined they'd be. "But Paul —"

He hushed her protest. "You said yourself that we can't waste time. Come on."

She grabbed her knapsack and followed Paul to the window. With a hard push on the sash, he was able to force the window open a few inches. Another firm push and it sprang open all the way. A blast of cold air hit their faces. "I'll help you out," he offered.

She peered down toward the rocks below the lighthouse. Everything looked white and serene in the moonlight. Yet the scene was eerily familiar. Remembering why, Susan froze.

Paul's hands were cupped at her foot, ready to assist her over the window ledge.

"No!" She gasped, clutching at his jacket. "Paul, this is the window where I saw Amy's face."

He tensed as she did, and his eyes met hers. "Are you sure?"

"I'm absolutely sure." Her gaze left his to travel over the room again. "Then this is where Travers held Amy hostage." The somber words were rhetorical, but the chill invading her bones made her shiver.

"We can't help Amy if we're dead."

The macabre truth of Paul's words prompted her to action. "We're not going to die," she said fiercely, bracing her hands on his shoulders for leverage. "Not when we've got —"

A noise from the hallway caused them both to stiffen.

"Travers!" They said it in panicky unison and there followed a moment of uncertainty before Paul shoved her in the direction of the window. "Get out, Susan!"

From the corner of her eye, she saw the door swing open. The glow from Travers's lantern clashed with the moonlight, catching her and Paul in the crossfire. Love and loyalty waged brief war in her heart with the desire to escape.

Travers's strident voice cursing them made no impression on Susan. Nor did

Paul's demand that she go. She knew that, as before, he would have no chance to follow her. And this time, her choice was very simple.

"I'm staying with you, Paul," she whispered, falling into his arms. Together they tumbled to the floor and landed right at Daryl Travers's combat-booted feet.

Chapter Thirteen

The other men swooped down on them like vultures, roughly pinning them to the floor. Susan heard the window slam shut; the curtains were drawn closed. Her knapsack was twisted from her hand and tossed aside.

Paul groaned. Susan watched as Rivera and Travers tied him up and carried him back across the room. Sully pulled the shoes off her feet and bound her ankles, then her wrists. She noticed he treated her with a certain gentleness. Their eyes met and she thought she saw regret in his. If only there were a way she could appeal to that shred of decency she sensed in him.

She knew Travers wouldn't allow her the opportunity. As he swaggered over to her, he looked like the fox who had cornered the hen and was about to move in for the kill.

"So it looks like our little lady reporter and her Prince Charming can't be trusted to behave themselves." He squatted down beside her, thrusting his face near hers.

She turned away from him, straining to see Paul. But Travers's hand came up to take hold of her chin. He jerked her head back so she was forced to look at him.

What she saw terrified her, though she tried valiantly not to show it. His eyes were full of hatred. His face wore an expression of triumph.

"Leave her alone."

The words, dripping ice, were Paul's. If she hadn't known better, Susan would have thought their fate had suddenly changed and he was the one giving the orders.

A muscle in Travers's chin twitched. It gave Susan the odd feeling that he had been momentarily shaken by Paul's bravery. There was dead silence in the room, then Travers rose suddenly. "You, shut up!" he roared, wagging a finger at Paul.

Paul's eyes made contact with hers. She wasn't sure how well he could see the love that she projected to him with her eyes and smile. But she saw clear evidence of his love for her, his contempt for Travers.

Travers whirled back to her, grabbing her under the arms. To her surprise, he dragged her over to where Paul lay and pitched her down beside him.

"Love and kisses time is over." Travers glowered at them, his face red with anger. "Before this night is through, you two are going to answer a few questions." He motioned to Sully, who was standing close by. "Watch them," he ordered tersely. Reaching in his pants pocket, he withdrew something and tossed it to Sully.

The object flashed silver in the light as Sully caught it. Susan saw it was a handgun. But instead of training the weapon on Paul and herself, Sully pointed it toward the floor. Choosing to believe that Sully was more embarrassed than eager to guard his defenseless prisoners, Susan ignored him and turned to Paul.

"We have to have faith. We can't give up, Paul," she whispered. How fervently she meant the words, but how hollow they sounded to her own ears!

His gaze held hers for a moment. Then he bowed his head, sighing. "Why didn't you at least try to go when you had the chance?"

Her vision blurred with tears. "I couldn't have made it." She believed that. Earlier she'd had hope that she might be able to escape and get help for Paul, but this time she wouldn't have gotten as far as Travers's gate.

"That's not the real reason," she added finally, touching her lips to his forehead. "I think you know that."

"I prayed you would get away, Susan." Tears misted his eyes too.

Snatches of their captors' conversation could be heard in the background. Travers and Rivera were arguing again, this time over when to kill their prisoners — after they finished questioning them or just before dawn at high tide. Trying desperately to block the gruesome subject from her mind, Susan determined that she and Paul must not waste whatever precious moments they had left.

"I didn't want a chance to escape, Paul. Not without you. Together, whether we're free or Travers's hostages, we have each other. If we live or if we . . ." She stopped short. A part of her rebelled against even voicing the possibility that she and Paul might die.

Paul kissed her temple. "Know what's wrong with you?" She shook her head. "Your heart's the hostage."

"Not just mine," she protested. It was true, perhaps even more so in his case. After all, he'd been ready to fall in love again; she'd had no desire for a serious relationship.

"Susan, there's . . ." Paul averted his eyes for a moment, then met hers again. "There's a question I need to ask you."

"What is it?"

"If we had the chance to . . . I mean, if we were able . . ." He cleared his throat. "How many children would you like to have?"

His question seemed almost absurd considering their very lives were in peril. Yet it touched Susan's heart deeply and she gave him a truthful answer. "I'd never thought too much about having children . . . until now. But if you wouldn't mind, that is, if you would be willing . . ." She hesitated only for a second. "I think four would be a nice number."

"I would be very willing." His smile was poignant. "And four suits me just fine."

The subject of children, of having his children, triggered a fierce determination in her. Was it her maternal instincts calling to her? Or was it the image of Amy Lambert's face that suddenly appeared in her mind? No matter, but it gave her another idea, one that had to work.

Travers was heading their way now. She had just enough time to whisper, "Paul, if I say something off the wall to Travers in the next several minutes, just go along with me. Okay?" His expression was one of puzzlement, but he said, "Okay," just before Travers reached them.

Travers held the knapsack in his hands. "Aren't we cozy." His sly glance slid from Paul to Susan as he unzipped the bag. "Let's see what we've got in here."

To Susan's chagrin, he pulled out the wire cutters. She glanced at Paul; he looked astonished.

"Planning on a bit of trespassing tonight?" Travers asked her with a smirk.

"You're very amusing, Mr. Travers." Susan mustered her best sarcastic smile.

Travers snorted and his eyes narrowed. "Just what *were* you planning to do?" He snarled the question.

"We had every right to be where we were. The fact is, we *didn't* trespass on your property," Paul offered firmly, as though he were in complete control of the situation.

Bolstered by Paul's outspokenness, Susan said, "Since you're so fond of questions, Mr. Travers, I might ask you one. Why did you kidnap Amy Lambert?"

Utter quiet filled the room. Travers's eyes grew wide, then darkly threatening. "Kidnap Amy Lambert? So that's your game. Take them!" he bellowed, jumping to his feet. He advanced on Rivera and Sully. "Take them out. You know what to do," he told the men with cold precision.

Rivera started across the room. When Sully held back, the third member of the *Mach III* crew, whose name Susan hadn't heard mentioned, jumped in. Susan felt the end was near. One look at Paul confirmed that he thought so too.

The men's boots thudded like the sound of doom on the wooden floor. With nothing more to lose, Susan called to Travers, "That wouldn't be a very smart thing for you to do, Mr. Travers. Killing us, I mean."

He rounded back on her. For a terrifying second, it seemed he would strike her with his raised fist.

"Sheriff Glendig is on his way. Now," she added as if she were never more sure of anything in her life.

Travers brought his face near hers. "You little liar!"

"It's true," Paul added. "He knows we were coming here."

"Liars! Both of you." Travers grabbed the gun away from Sully and fired it into the air. Then, with a swift gesture, he brought his other hand up and dealt a blow to Paul's cheek.

The scream that filled the room was Susan's, though she was barely aware of it. She lunged at Travers, fighting savagely to get her hands loose. It was hopeless.

With one swift move, Travers pinned her against the wall. His fingers gripped her hair, yanking her head back. "You think you can mess with me, do you?" he challenged.

Susan could only cry out. Pain seared her scalp where her hair was held taut.

Paul cried her name; she moaned in response. Travers was bent on driving them mad. It must be part of his plan. First torture, then kill his victims.

But the next moment, chaos reigned in the room. The door burst open, cracking on its hinges. A voice barked, "Hold it! Get your hands in the air!"

Susan knew she must be hallucinating. Travers broke from her, leaping up. Curses flew and something else — gunfire. Two shots rang out, perhaps three. Then silence.

"Hands above your heads, now!" came the order again. Susan recognized the voice this time, but she still couldn't believe what was happening. With shocked amazement, she turned and saw the lanky form of the sheriff standing in the center of the room. He held a rifle in his hands that was pointed at Daryl Travers. The sheriff wasn't alone. Two men in uniform flanked him.

Her eyes traveled to Rivera, Sully, and the third accomplice. All the bravado seemed gone from the men. Rivera was clutching his left arm.

"You did tell Sheriff Glendig, after all."

Paul was talking to her. She looked at him. He appeared equally stunned, but more, it seemed, for the fact that her prediction had come true so quickly. "No." She shook her head. "I made that up. I wonder how he could have —"

She was interrupted by one of the men in uniform, a deputy no doubt. He bent down and cut the ropes binding her wrists and ankles. After helping her to her feet, he freed Paul.

Paul pulled her into his arms and they watched as handcuffs were slapped on Travers and the others, all except for Rivera, who must have taken one of the bullets. The sheriff gave the order for the new prisoners to be escorted out, then he gave his attention to Paul and Susan.

"I'm surprised to find you two in Travers's lighthouse, but maybe I shouldn't be." He frowned. "Are you all right?"

"We are now that you're here," Paul said.

The sheriff regarded Paul thoughtfully. "Looks like you got knocked around. Travers?"

Paul nodded. "And the others."

"I'll take statements from both of you in a couple of minutes, as soon as I see our new prisoners safely on their way." Sheriff Glendig started for the door.

"How did you know to come?" Susan had to ask the question.

The law officer stopped and turned around. "I didn't come to rescue you. We had other business with Travers." He directed his remarks at Susan. She wondered if that "other business" had to do with Amy Lambert. But before she could summon the courage to ask, the sheriff added, "It's the Coast Guard that's hunting for you."

"The Coast Guard?" she and Paul repeated at once.

The sheriff crossed his arms. "Sam called me a couple of hours ago. Said he'd noticed the *Anne Marie* had gone out, but hadn't come back. He was worried about you. A lucky thing, wouldn't you say?" He didn't wait for a reply before he strode from the room.

Susan looked at Paul. "I remember

thinking not long ago that Sam would be a good man to have around if I was ever in trouble."

"You were right. But what about the sheriff?" Paul raised his eyebrows.

She was forced to admit, "Yes, he's a good man too. A very good man."

With a smile, Paul drew her closer. It was exactly where she needed to be. "I'm glad to hear your confession."

Returning his smile, Susan wrapped her arms around his neck. "I hate to say so, but I misjudged Sheriff Glendig."

"Then there's no more contention between us on that point?"

"Definitely not, though I doubt the man will ever be above embarrassing me with his questions," she said, half teasing before her lips met Paul's.

The kiss was more one of celebration than passion. At that moment, there was much to celebrate. They were still alive, and they had each other. Leaning back, Paul declared, "What a story this is all going to make."

"The one we lived to tell about. But are we up to writing it?"

Paul grinned. "I think we can manage somehow. A true eyewitness account." Then, in a more practical vein, he said,

"We have to find your waders."

With a sigh, she pulled away from him. "Yes. I'd hate to think one of Travers's men stashed them on the *Mach III*."

Susan first retrieved her wire cutters, grateful that Paul didn't question her about them. As they combed the room looking for her waders, she told him, "I want you to see a doctor about your injuries."

"I'm fine," he insisted. The cut on his forehead, the bruise on his cheek, told a different story.

"I still want you to get checked out. Does Gull Harbor have a doctor?"

Paul grinned again. "Two, matter of fact. I promise I'll have one of them check me out, right after I see about a new pair of glasses." He bent down by the sofa. "Wait! I think there may be something under here."

Susan knelt down beside him. He reached under the dust ruffle. But he didn't pull out her waders.

It was a small stuffed bear wearing a striped vest. One of its eyes was missing and there was a tear in the fake fur on its stomach that exposed the stuffing.

"How do you suppose . . ." He didn't finish the question.

She took the toy from him and held it in her hands. "Travers bought it for Amy from Anna's shop?"

Paul studied the toy. "Yes, that's possible."

The sheriff came back then. They both rose and met him by the door. "I presume these belong to you, Susan." He held up her waders. She must have looked pleased, for he smiled. "They were out in the hallway."

"I have something for you too, Sheriff Glendig." She accepted her boots from him and gave him the bear.

"What's this?" He turned it over in his hands.

"We were looking for the waders and found the toy under the sofa," Paul explained.

The sheriff nodded but made no comment. He took their statements and lectured them on the dangers of trying to play detective. Then he told them the Coast Guard would tow the *Anne Marie* back to the marina. One of his deputies would take them home.

After they had expressed their gratitude for his timely, if unexpected, rescue, Susan and Paul accompanied him out and got into the back of the one car that was empty. Travers and his men occupied the backseats of the other squad cars.

As they settled beside each other, Paul draped his arm around her. Susan gazed out the window and saw that the moon had disappeared. She peered toward the water below. Nothing was visible, though she could hear the roar of the waves against the rocks.

A nightmare image crossed her mind — of herself and Paul lying cold and silent at the bottom of some frigid bay. She shivered and Paul whispered his concern. "I'm all right," she assured him.

As if he wasn't quite convinced, he nestled her protectively in his arms all the way home.

Some time later, they sat on the deck of Susan's cottage. Neither had been able to sleep, though both of them were exhausted. Together they watched the sky gradually change from an impersonal shade of gray to warm crimson.

"I don't know when I've ever seen a more beautiful sunrise, Paul."

"Neither have I." He leaned over to softly nuzzle her hair.

Turning to look at him, Susan was pleased that his coloring had improved.

She had bathed and treated the cut on his forehead. Now it was barely noticeable, though the bruise on his cheek stood out. He wore a slight frown as he watched her. He might be feeling better, but it seemed she couldn't hide her own troubling thoughts from him.

"What is it?" Paul touched her cheek.

"I'm not sure." She hesitated. "You'll think I'm crazy."

"You know better than that. Tell me," he coaxed.

"I was so certain Travers had taken Amy Lambert. There seems to be even more reason to believe that now."

"But you don't?"

Averting her eyes, Susan gazed out over the water. The foamy crests of the waves looked as if they'd been frosted with pink icing. She rose abruptly. When Paul started to follow, she put a hand on his shoulder. "Wait here. I'll only be inside a minute."

She came back with one of the bears she'd bought at Anna's shop and handed it to Paul. "I haven't come up with a name for him. What do you think would be appropriate?"

He regarded the bear solemnly. "I'm not very good with names."

"That's all right. Maybe Anna can help me." She took the bear from him. "For some reason I can't get Anna out of my mind." Susan shook her head. "Maybe it's the way she looked when I asked her about Amy Lambert. She seemed so frightened the day Travers came into Bears' Tea Party. Then, at the estuary, after my run-in with Travers, you told me that Anna's property borders his."

"You don't think there's a connection?" Paul sounded skeptical.

"I said you'd believe I was crazy."

"No. Intelligent, perceptive. Let's see. Yes, and very, very beautiful."

How many times could she hear those words and never tire of them? Forever hardly seemed long enough. She had a terrible urge to dissolve into his arms and stay there a while, but she stifled it. "Your vote of confidence is greatly appreciated." She smiled. "Maybe I wouldn't be so uneasy if Bears' Tea Party hadn't suddenly gone up for sale."

"Exactly what are you trying to say, Susan?"

She reached for his hand. Holding it in hers, she traced the few small calluses that marred his palm. His eyes closed briefly. "Could we talk to her — Anna, that is? If she knows something about Amy's disappearance, or about Travers's activities, maybe we could persuade her to tell Sheriff Glendig."

To her surprise, Paul got up, pulling her with him. "We should be able to catch her at home this morning."

"Not this early?" Susan looked at her watch; it read half past seven.

"No. We'll wait until about nine, a decent hour by most people's standards."

She knew he was teasing her. "Even mine," she retorted.

"You'll have to drive."

"What about your promise to see the doctor, not to mention getting new glasses?"

"Let's go to Anna's place first. Then if you're really in the mood to play taxi driver, you can take me to the doctor's office and the optical shop. I give very good tips," he added, drawing her into a kiss.

"I'll say," she replied with a sigh when their lips finally parted.

Chapter Fourteen

As soon as Susan saw Anna Winston's face, she knew her intuition had been right. Anna was hiding something.

The older woman had opened her front door to her visitors only after several persistent knocks, and then little more than a crack.

Anna's neat bungalow was at the end of a long lane. To Susan, the place seemed isolated and lonely, not unlike Travers's lighthouse. The idea that Anna's closest neighbor might be Travers himself gave Susan a chill.

"Good morning, Anna," Paul offered when no one else spoke.

Anna's head bobbed in greeting. "Paul . . . Susan." She sounded out of breath, as if she'd been hurrying. "I'm . . . sorry. I wasn't expecting company."

"We know you weren't," Susan said. She searched for the right words to put Anna at ease. "And we didn't mean to frighten you."

"Frighten?" Anna's eyes grew larger. "What makes you think you frightened me?"

The question might have been amusing under different circumstances. Ignoring it, Susan said, "We'd like to talk to you, Anna. Just for a few minutes."

The older woman wavered visibly.

"It's very important," Paul put in, resting his hand on Susan's shoulder.

Anna cleared her throat. "Well, I'd very much enjoy visiting with you both, but —" She let out a sudden cry. "What happened to you, Paul?" Her mouth gaped open as she stared at his bruised face.

He shrugged. "A . . . an accident. I'm fine, Anna."

Susan saw her opportunity. "Not exactly an accident, Anna. What happened to Paul is part of why we need to talk to you. About Amy Lambert," she added firmly.

"About . . . Amy?" the older woman stammered, eyes darting from Paul to Susan.

"We have a story to tell you, Anna, a true one," Susan went on. "Please, may we come in?"

A silence followed. Then Anna drew back the door. "All right," she said wearily.

After stepping inside, Susan saw the

living room was cluttered with packing boxes. And bears. On every available piece of furniture sat a toy bear.

"I'm afraid there's no place to sit," Anna offered apologetically.

Susan had the notion it was a convenient excuse. "That's okay."

"We can stand," Paul said from behind her.

"You're getting ready to move." Susan got a small nod from Anna in acknowledgement. "We were surprised and sorry to see you'd put Bears' Tea Party up for sale."

The older woman's mouth twisted into a nervous smile. "Yes, dear. I've decided to return to North Carolina."

"Isn't this kind of quick?" The question was Paul's. "Wasn't your shop doing well?"

"Well enough to pay the bills." Anna's tongue flicked over her lips. "I guess I've become suddenly homesick." She fell silent, gazing at the floor.

Susan decided it was time to get to the real reason for their visit. "Paul told me you used to baby-sit for Chris Lambert." Anna's head jerked up. "You don't think Amy is dead, do you?"

Anna sucked in a sharp breath. "Dead? Dear Susan, don't talk like that."

Susan felt Paul's hand take hold of hers. "What Susan means is that you believe Amy's alive, maybe even close by."

Anna vigorously shook her head. "No . . . that is, I do want to believe she's alive. But it was her father who stole her, that terrible man." Her eyes beseeched Susan's.

Susan took a step toward the older woman, tugging at Paul's hand to follow. "I'm going to tell you a story, Anna. It's a true tale that happened to Paul and me last night. The ugly bruise on his cheek, the cut on his forehead. . . . Daryl Travers did that."

Anna's hands flew to her face in horror even as she retreated a step. "No!"

"Yes, and it was because we had gone too near his precious lighthouse. Do you have any idea why we risked our lives going there?"

Anna shook her head again.

"Not very long ago, I saw a child's face at one of the windows in the abandoned keeper's quarters."

"A child's face?" Anna repeated hoarsely.

"Amy Lambert's."

"That's impossible!" Anna wrung her hands together, withdrawing another step from her visitors.

"I couldn't forget that little face," Susan replied adamantly. "I'd seen Amy's picture in a copy of the paper that Paul gave me." Cautiously she approached Anna. "I thought Travers was holding Amy hostage, so Paul and I went back to Rocky Pointe to search for her. Travers and his men took us prisoners, that is, until Sheriff Glendig rescued us."

"We're okay," Paul assured Anna, reaching out to touch the older woman's arm.

"Yes. He and his deputies came to arrest Travers. We don't know why, but Daryl Travers is in jail now. He can't hurt anyone," Susan emphasized, praying the news would loosen Anna's tongue.

"Thank goodness," Anna whispered. Her eyes closed briefly.

"But no trace of Amy was found in the lighthouse, except . . ." Susan walked over and picked up a small bear similar to the one Paul had discovered. "We found a bear much like this one hidden under the sofa in the room where Travers held us. The room where Amy's face had appeared at the window."

"Stop!" Anna pleaded, putting her hands to her ears.

"Susan."

It was Paul, sounding slightly on edge, who alerted Susan that she was pressing Anna too hard. Yet she couldn't hold back what she had to say. "That day, my first one in town, Travers came into Bears' Tea Party. He scared you in some way. I saw the fear in your eyes after he left. You know something, don't you? Information about Amy's disappearance. Please tell us, Anna. No, please tell the sheriff." In a reassuring voice, she added, "I promise that Travers can't hurt you."

"It's all right, Susan." Paul's voice was soothing. His hand squeezed hers until it hurt.

"No, it isn't."

Susan wasn't sure who gasped the loudest: Anna, Paul, or herself. All three turned sharply toward a doorway that led off the living room. There stood a petite, blond-haired woman. She was dressed in a white sweater and a long, flowing skirt.

Susan recognized the face from somewhere, but she wasn't prepared for the shock that came when Paul went over to the woman.

"Chris!" he exclaimed.

"Chris," Susan echoed. "Chris Lambert?"

The woman came across the room. "Yes."

Susan noted then how very young Chris Lambert was — and how very anxious she looked. Susan saw something else. There was a slight movement from behind the woman's skirt. A small face peered suddenly around the folds of cloth.

"Amy!" The exclamation came from Susan and Paul at once. *Could it really be?* Susan watched in awe as the blond child, a delicate copy of her mother, stepped away from her hiding place to look wonderingly at the other adults. In her arms she clutched the large white bear that had occupied the window of Anna's shop, the one Anna had said was spoken for.

Paul immediately crouched in front of the child. "Don't be scared, Amy. We're friends of your mommy's. We're your friends too."

Amy turned huge eyes on her mother.

Chris knelt beside her daughter. "Paul's right, Amy. They're our friends."

Susan wished she could see Chris's face, but a curtain of hair shielded the young woman's expression.

"You should have stayed back, Chris. You and the child should have waited."

Anna's anguished voice drew Susan's attention back to the older woman, nearly forgotten in the shock of finding Amy safe.

More than safe. Alive and well in the company of her mother. Not Sean Lambert.

"No, Anna. No more hiding."

Chris sounded determined, but relief was soon overcome in Susan's mind by questions about Amy's disappearance and sudden return. She wasn't sure how many would ever be answered. She sent Paul a help signal with her eyes, but he was occupied with Amy. He had the child smiling, talking in low tones as he pointed to the bear's bow tie.

The scene made Susan think of a conversation she and Paul had had a short time ago and her mind took another turn. *Yes, he would make a very good father one day,* she thought.

"I know what we did was wrong."

Susan's attention refocused on Chris.

"I just wanted what was best for them. I love them." Anna began to sob and Susan turned to put her arm around the older woman's shoulders.

"Of course you do," Susan soothed. Mingled with the relief and puzzlement she felt was compassion for a lonely woman who so obviously adored the young mother and child.

"Don't blame Anna. She only did what I asked."

"Chris, I'm not sure blame is the right word for what's apparently happened here." That was from Paul. He came up beside Susan, holding Amy and the bear in his arms.

"I know what this poor child went through." Anna indicated she meant Chris. "My husband abused me too. It was many years ago, but I never forgot the . . . the terror I felt." Anna shivered visibly. "Thank goodness I never had any children of my own," she added in a whisper.

The revelation stirred even more sympathy in Susan for both Anna and Chris. "You staged the kidnapping, didn't you, Chris?" she asked quietly. It seemed nearly impossible that the frail-looking young woman could have fooled the authorities. Yet she obviously had.

Chris averted her eyes. "Yes. I was so afraid."

"Afraid of Sean?" Paul prompted.

"He didn't have visiting rights. He'd never asked for them," Chris said hastily. "But he was around, and after the divorce was final, he made several threats."

Susan remembered something else she'd read in the article on Amy's kidnapping. "But didn't Sean leave the area?"

"That's what the authorities concluded,"

Chris acknowledged. "I hoped that if he had finally left, he wouldn't come back. I wanted him to be the one running scared."

"Did you tell Sheriff Glendig about the threats?" Before her change of heart about the law officer, Susan might not have asked the question.

"I talked with him, yes. But there really wasn't anything he could do. Sean was, *is,* a very determined man. I had feared for Amy's safety for so long. If Sean wanted her badly enough . . ." Chris broke off. In a trembling voice, she pleaded, "Can you understand why I had to do something?"

"You and Amy came to Anna's to stay." The statement was redundant, but Susan considered the implications. Chris had told the authorities she had gone to live with relatives.

"We hadn't planned to be here long." Chris gazed with affection at the older woman.

"Dear child, you wouldn't have had anywhere else to go." Anna put her arm around Chris and gave Amy a kiss. The little girl reached for her; Paul turned her over to Anna's care.

Susan gently asked Chris, "You don't have any other family?"

"Not except for an uncle in Wisconsin. I

haven't seen him in years." She smiled sadly. "My mother died when I was eight. She and Dad had divorced when I was one." Sighing, she went on, "My grandparents died years before I was born."

There was silence in the room until Susan whispered, "I'm sorry."

Clearing his throat, Paul said, "You realize that what you've done is serious, Chris."

"Yes." She appeared resigned. "It's funny, but just yesterday I told Anna I couldn't let her cover for us any longer. You know she's got the shop up for sale?" Chris shook her head. "She was planning on taking us with her to North Carolina."

"You deserve a chance at a new life," Anna put in fiercely, like a mother hen defending her chicks.

"It's all right," Chris said softly, patting Anna's hand.

"Chris, you'll have to go to the sheriff and tell him the truth."

"I know, Paul." Apprehension passed over Chris's face.

"I'll go with you, if you want."

"Thanks, Paul. I'd appreciate that a lot."

Susan threw Paul an "I love you" look. Their eyes locked for a moment. Then, turning to Chris, she said, "You're doing the right thing. But how did Amy come to be in the lighthouse? I didn't imagine her face that day."

"I was bad. I runned away!"

The pronouncement came from Amy. She beamed at Susan, then her mother.

"That's right. You did, and you gave me a terrible scare," her mother said in rebuke.

"How did you get inside the big lighthouse?" Paul asked the child.

"Through the fence."

"She really means the gate," Chris explained. "It was open."

Susan considered that Travers must have gotten careless — or had been expecting a visit from the crew of the *Mach III*.

"When I saw that she was gone," Chris continued, taking Amy from Anna, "I thought that Sean had found us and gotten her. I was frantic. Then I found a path at the edge of the woods behind Anna's backyard. Not knowing what else to do, I followed it, calling out for Amy. The path ended just outside Travers's property."

"I've been on that path myself," Paul said. "It's one of a number of hiking trails that border the cliffs."

Chris nodded. "I got as far as the gate

when I saw Amy running toward me from the lighthouse." She kissed her daughter's cheek.

Susan shivered, thinking how close Amy had come to being caught by Travers. "You were lucky, Chris. About the time you found her, Travers was confronting me on the rocks just below his property." She didn't mention that he was carrying a rifle. "Did you lose a teddy bear inside the lighthouse, Amy?"

The child looked surprised for a moment. Then she shook her head vigorously. "Didn't lose," she said softly, clutching the white bear closer to herself.

Susan wasn't prepared for the negative response. It took her a moment to recover. "Are you sure, Amy?" The child shook her head once more. Susan gave her attention to Chris. "We found a small teddy bear under a sofa in the room where Travers held us. We thought it belonged to Amy, so we gave it to Sheriff Glendig."

"And speaking of the sheriff," Paul said before Chris could respond, "he should be in his office by now. Susan and I can take you back to town with us."

"I'm going too," Anna put in quickly. She folded her arms in a determined way.

Still wondering about the bear and how

it ended up under Travers's sofa, Susan said, "I've got room for three in the backseat."

"Since my glasses were lost in the wrestling match with Travers, Susan is playing taxi driver," Paul added with a rueful smile.

Anna suddenly pressed her fingers to her temples, as she had the day Travers was in her shop. "That awful man," she declared.

Chris took hold of Anna's hand. "Don't worry," she urged. "Everything's going to be all right."

Susan said a silent prayer that it would.

Then, squaring her thin shoulders, Chris turned to Susan and Paul. "We're ready to go, if you are."

The next Tuesday, Susan sat beside Paul on the same bench they'd occupied before at Barr Estuary. The day was sunny; the air, brisk. The uppermost leaves on the cluster of oak and maple trees at the water's edge had turned shades of brown and scarlet.

Autumn had arrived. Yet the thought that winter was not far off, with its gray days and frequent snow squalls, didn't depress Susan as it usually did. Instead, she looked forward to the change in seasons. She felt more optimistic than she had in some time — about life in general and her life in particular. She credited the man beside her with that.

That man had just piqued her curiosity. Not only was she anxious for an update on Daryl Travers's case as well as how Chris and Amy were doing, she couldn't wait to see the latest issue of the *Gull Beacon*. Was that what Paul had in the large sack he'd brought with him?

He placed it on the ground beside the bench. "Okay, so what's in there?" Susan pointed at the sack.

"Later." He grinned at her pouting expression as he slipped an arm firmly around her waist, drawing her close.

Susan observed him, a favorite activity of late. The bruise on his cheek was fading; the cut on his forehead was healing nicely. "You're feeling better?"

"Yes. Thanks to Dr. Dobson and you."

"I'm flattered, but I've had little to do with your recovery." She didn't add an "I told you so," even if Dr. Dobson *had* confirmed her suspicions that Paul had suffered a very mild concussion.

"You had everything to do with it," Paul insisted. "All that T.L.C. you gave me."

"Well, the doctor did say bed rest for a day or two."

"But he didn't prescribe kisses and chicken soup," Paul teased. He leaned back and she admired the view some more. He wore his new pair of glasses.

Though she'd helped him pick out the tortoise-shell frames, assuring him many times how much she liked them, he had seemed uncertain about the choice.

Frowning slightly, Paul removed the glasses and eyed them critically. "You really think these are okay? Maybe I should have gotten contacts."

"No." She took the glasses from him and fitted them back over the bridge of his nose. "You look very . . . ah, handsome, Paul." He squirmed and she laughed. "I mean it. And every inch the newspaperman, I might add."

This time he laughed. "You're flattering me."

"Not at all," she protested, taking his face in her hands. She kissed him before he had a chance to reply. Then, resting her head on his shoulder, she asked, "Are you going to tell me what happened yesterday while I was toiling in Pitston or let me die of curiosity?" Necessity had dictated that she attend the mayors' conference while

260

Paul prepared a particularly sensational issue of the *Beacon*.

"Lots happened yesterday." His short reply caused her to draw back to look at him. "For starters, Detective Osborn got a positive I.D. on the fingerprint found on your door."

Susan clutched at his arm. "Who?"

"Marion Travers."

Susan's mouth fell open. "Marion? Why?"

"She was trying to find your camera."

"My camera?"

"Apparently her brother was afraid you'd taken a picture of something at his lighthouse, something he wouldn't care for the sheriff to see."

"Evidence, maybe?"

Paul nodded. "The break-in at your cottage was staged. But, under questioning, Sully broke down and confessed that he and the rest of the *Mach III* crew were responsible for the burglaries in the Quay Road area."

"Stealing things, selling them on the black market," Susan guessed.

"Yes. And bigger game. They were into smuggling drugs." Paul paused. "In teddy bears," he added emphatically.

"Bears!" She sat up straight. "In *Anna's* bears?"

Paul nodded solemnly. "She didn't know, of course. He told her the stuffed animals were for his mother."

"Don't you think Anna must have been suspicious?"

"Obviously she did wonder, but she wasn't about to question him on the point." Paul's mouth curved in a small smile.

"I see what you mean," Susan acknowledged, remembering her own attempts at questioning Travers.

"Anna told Sheriff Glendig that Travers never seemed interested in the bears on display in her shop. She had to special-order them for him from a dealer in Boston." Paul looked away for a moment. Then he continued. "There was a delay in one of the shipments. Travers took his frustration out on Anna."

"The day I saw him in her shop."

"That's right. But drugs and hot property weren't Travers's only vices. Anna gave the sheriff some information that prompted Travers to confess to another crime." Paul paused.

"What?" Susan clutched his arm.

"Blackmail. Anna herself was the victim."

Susan drew in a sharp breath. The sun's

warmth seemed gone. "Why would he do that? Other than hiding Chris and Amy, poor Anna didn't have . . ." Her voice trailed off.

"You just said it," Paul interjected. "When Amy ran away to the lighthouse, Travers saw her. Without their knowledge, he followed Chris and Amy along the trail back to Anna's house."

Hatred wasn't a strong enough word for the way Susan felt toward Daryl Travers. How could one man cause so much misery for so many people? "No wonder Anna put the shop up for sale so fast. And it was a Higgins Agency sign in the window."

"That was part of the scheme. He and his fair sister planned to clean up on the profits. Marion could easily doctor a contract."

"Anna was planning to leave, though, wasn't she? She and Chris and Amy?"

"She was. Chris still isn't aware of the blackmail scheme, but she will be when she reads the write-up in the paper." Paul pulled Susan around so they were fully facing each other. "Anna tried to protect Chris and Amy. If Travers had had his way, she would have left town a lot poorer."

"It's so terrible." Susan was worried about the older woman. Could she endure the stress of possibly having to testify in court? "Did you see Anna yesterday?"

"Yes." Paul brushed back a strand of hair from Susan's cheek. "She's holding up okay. Anna's been through a lot in her life, but one of the most important things now is that she'll be able to keep her shop. That is, if she wants to."

"I think she will. How could she give up all of her bears?"

"You mean her children," Paul corrected, not for the first time.

Susan's laughter was bittersweet.

"What is it?" Paul coaxed. His hands slid down over her shoulders, squeezing gently.

"Nothing, just . . . I wish that Joey had been found safe, that his story had a happy ending."

"Susan, not all stories have happy endings." Paul's quiet words drew her eyes to his. "We have to be grateful for the ones that do. I am."

Susan swallowed back tears. She knew he must be thinking of Andrea. Once, she'd questioned whether she reminded Paul of Andrea, if that was the reason he'd been so strongly attracted to her. But she no longer felt any need to ask. She couldn't doubt Paul's love for her, not after everything they'd been through together.

Finally she said, "You're right, Paul."

In the silence a hawk cried out. Susan lifted her eyes to the sky, searching for him. "I heard him when we were here before."

"Yes, a goshawk. He likes to sit there." Paul pointed to a branch on a nearby tree.

"I can't see him." At least she had her camera today.

"He'll be around shortly. And it looks like his sanctuary is secure for the present."

Susan regarded Paul with surprise. "You mean Harlan Brown backed out?"

"Backed out and left town, licking his wounds."

Susan laughed, a hearty, joyous laugh. But soon her thoughts turned serious again. "What do you think will happen to Chris?"

"I don't know," Paul said honestly, though his smile was comforting. "Try not to worry too much. Sheriff Glendig is a compassionate man. By now, I'm sure he has a better idea of the kind of desperation Chris felt. She's very young, very much alone, and very afraid. I have faith that the authorities will take all of that into account."

"Are Chris and Amy still at Ruth Westman's?" They'd been escorted there after

Chris's initial meeting with the sheriff. He'd told Chris to stay in town.

"Yes, safe and protected."

Paul's answer banished Susan's idea that the sheriff might have changed his mind and put Chris in jail.

"And there's a promising lead on Sean Lambert's whereabouts," Paul added.

"Really? Where?" Susan prayed it was someplace faraway.

"Canada. Ontario."

"Just as the sheriff figured."

Paul let go of her for a moment, then he bent over and retrieved the sack. "You were curious about this?"

"Extremely," Susan teased.

He fished in the sack and drew out a folded newspaper. "First copy off the press," he announced, handing it to her with a flourish.

"All the gruesome details," she quipped as she stared at the front page. Travers's arrest was splashed in bold headlines across the top. There were pictures of the man himself and his accomplices. "Nice mug shots."

Paul grinned. "I thought you'd like them."

A picture of Amy was farther down the page. "You took this?" Paul nodded. "This is worth everything," Susan whispered, touching the photo of the smiling child.

"I know." Paul's face wore a look of satisfaction.

Scanning the article, Susan saw her own name mentioned about halfway down the first column. The word "heroine" followed closely. "Heroine?" she asked, disbelieving.

"I'm not the only one who thinks so. Just ask the sheriff."

"Now you're the one doing the flattering, Paul Stuart. The sheriff never said that."

"Maybe not in so many words, but he did say you're plucky."

"*Plucky?*"

Paul ducked his head in an attempt to hide his expression from her. She took hold of his chin, forcing him to face her. He looked sheepish. "Translate that to 'stupid,' Paul."

"I choose to call you a heroine and it stands," Paul replied stubbornly.

"And I don't suppose the newspaper editor is just the least bit prejudiced?"

Paul feigned a look of offense. "You're accusing me of biased reporting? And just when I was about to say how much better a newspaper the *Beacon* would be if it were a

Mom and Pop operation." He dropped the sack. It landed with a thud on the ground, telling Susan the paper wasn't the only thing he'd been hiding from her.

But his last remark had so riveted her attention that she let the subject of the sack's contents slide. "Mom and Pop?" It sounded homey — like the village of Gull Harbor itself. "That might work."

"Yes. Stuart and Stuart, editors. An equal partnership."

Susan wrapped her arms around his neck. "I think I like the idea. And in due time, we might expand the operation."

"By four."

So when he'd asked her how many children she wanted, the question hadn't been born solely out of their desperate plight. He'd really wanted to know. There was another matter just as important to her. "About my research, Paul. I don't want to give that up."

"I don't want you to." With obvious reluctance, he released her and picked up the sack again. "That brings us to my other surprise." He reached in and pulled out a pair of boots.

No, not boots. "Swamp waders!" Susan couldn't conceal her delight.

Paul chuckled. "You're the only woman I

know who could get excited over an ugly pair of boots."

It was her turn to act offended. "They're not boots. And they're not ugly. They're beautiful." She had a sudden vision of Paul and herself tramping through some remote corner of the estuary, waders on, camera and notebook at the ready. But the image had a slight flaw.

"What's wrong? You're frowning." Paul looked suddenly concerned. "You don't wish you could explore tide pools with Rodney Silvers instead, do you?"

Susan regarded him with astonishment. "How could you even think such a thing? You know better than that!" she chided. But she couldn't hide a smile.

Paul was instantly contrite. "I'm sorry."

It was apparent to her that she hadn't been the only one with doubts. At the same time, she felt a little flattered.

After a moment Paul said, "I wasn't sure if I should tell you, but I might as well. I understand that Rodney's gone south."

"South? I hadn't heard."

Paul acted mildly amazed. "He's moved to Miami to open a new branch of his father's seafood sauce company."

"It figures." That was all Susan said, though she could have guessed Rodney's destination. "Enough of that subject," she said firmly. "The reason I was frowning was because occasionally I see you in a different way."

Paul appeared intrigued, "You mean other than a newspaper editor?"

"Something *more* than an editor. Here . . ." She opened the paper to the inside pages and located what she was looking for. "The Closet Poet," she said, glancing sideways at Paul to see his reaction. He shifted a bit uncomfortably.

But when she saw the title of that week's poem, a lump filled her throat. " 'Hostage Hearts,' " she said under her breath. Half the poem she read to herself; the other half she read aloud.

With silent hope, a step beyond
the tender tides that mark the dawn,
We wait. We watch the restless sea,
the moaning wind that fades to breeze;
The endless winding of the day
in hands that hold eternity,
Until the bitter storm has passed
and hostage hearts are free at last.

She threw her arms around Paul, almost knocking him off balance in her enthusiasm. "That was beautiful, K. Garnett."

Recovering nicely, he kissed her in a passionate manner — as a poet would. "You knew, Susan."

"When I read your last poem, yes. I was sure it had been written just for me."

"It was."

A sharp, vibrant cry made them both turn their heads. There on the branch sat the goshawk, just as Paul had promised.

He was a magnificent bird, all raw power and regal intelligence. In her haste, Susan fumbled for her camera. It fell from her hands.

Paul swiftly saved it for her.

"I don't want to scare him away," she whispered.

"You won't," Paul whispered back. "Here, let me help you." His hands grasped her shoulders, guiding her around to a more favorable position. "He'll pose like that for a long time." Paul's breath was hot on her neck; his mouth nuzzled her ear.

He'd better, Susan thought, adrift for a moment in the sensation Paul was creating with his lips on her skin. But as she focused her camera on the hawk, she felt another kind of thrill. The bird remained completely still, as if he understood she was about to take the perfect picture.

The employees of Thorndike Press hope you have enjoyed this Large Print book. All our Thorndike and Wheeler Large Print titles are designed for easy reading, and all our books are made to last. Other Thorndike Press Large Print books are available at your library, through selected bookstores, or directly from us.

For information about titles, please call:

(800) 223-1244

or visit our Web site at:

www.gale.com/thorndike
www.gale.com/wheeler

To share your comments, please write:

Publisher
Thorndike Press
295 Kennedy Memorial Drive
Waterville, ME   04901